HAVE BODY WILL GUARD:
TEACH ME TONIGHT

Neil Plakcy

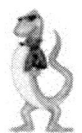

Dedication

To Marc: always and forever.

Acknowledgement

Thanks to all the wonderful folks at Loose Id for helping me bring Aidan and Liam to life and to readers. Special thanks to Irene Williams and Maryam Salim, who have provided so much helpful input.

Praise for the *Have Body Will Guard* series

Three Wrong Turns in the Desert
A Lambda Literary Award Finalist

"This book was a real joy to read and I'm thrilled to have discovered the writing of Neil Plakcy."
— Kathy, *Dark Diva Reviews*

"*Three Wrong Turns in the Desert* is one wild ride for the readers. This one is definitely a keeper…
— Sandra, *Night Owl Reviews*

Dancing with the Tide

"…you won't be able to put *Dancing With The Tide* down until you finish the story."
— Lydia, *Rainbow Reviews*

"…a treat and a half! Neil Plakcy has done it again…"
— Kathy K., *Reviews at Ebook Addict*

Teach Me Tonight

"A heart pounding romantic drama that keeps readers on their toes, Teach Me Tonight doesn't disappoint."
— Lisa, *Joyfully Reviewed*

"…a very entertaining book that will hold your attention from the first page to the last."
— *Literary Nymphs*

Loose Id®

ISBN 13: 978-1-61118-395-5
HAVE BODY WILL GUARD: TEACH ME TONIGHT
Copyright © April 2012 by Neil Plakcy
Originally released in e-book format in June 2011

Cover Art by April Martinez
Cover Layout and Design by April Martinez

All rights reserved. Except for use of brief quotations in any review or critical article, the reproduction or utilization of this work in whole or in part in any form by any electronic, mechanical or other means, now known or hereafter invented, including xerography, photo-copying and recording, or in any information storage or retrieval is forbidden without the prior written permission of Loose Id LLC, PO Box 809, San Francisco CA 94104-0809. http://www.loose-id.com

DISCLAIMER: Many of the acts described in our BDSM/fetish titles can be dangerous. Please do not try any new sexual practice, whether it be fire, rope, or whip play, without the guidance of an experienced practitioner. Neither Loose Id nor its authors will be responsible for any loss, harm, injury or death resulting from use of the information contained in any of its titles.

This book is an original publication of Loose Id. Each individual story herein was previously published in e-book format only by Loose Id and is a work of fiction. Any similarity to actual persons, events or existing locations is entirely coincidental.

Printed in the U.S.A. by
Lightning Source, Inc.
1246 Heil Quaker Blvd
La Vergne TN 37086
www.lightningsource.com

Chapter One

Aidan Greene stood at the foot of a staircase in the Stade Olympique El Menzah as a hot sirocco blew through the northern suburbs of Tunis. It brought with it a fine coating of sand, which stung Aidan's face. He turned sideways to avoid the brunt of the wind, but there was no escaping the hot June sun, which beat mercilessly down on the stadium and the two soccer teams on the field.

The Carthage Eagles led the Millwall Football Club by three goals. Millwall had a reputation for having some of the most dangerous supporters of any soccer club, and that had prompted the organizers of the exhibition game to hire as much security as they could.

Looking around the stadium, Aidan recognized several other bodyguards who regularly worked in Tunis. Liam McCullough, his partner in love and business, stood a few hundred feet away, guarding a different staircase. Off-duty officers were stationed at each exit, wearing white pinneys with POLICE printed on the front and back.

The mostly male crowd was yelling obscenities at the field, shaking fists and waving placards imprinted with the club's logo of a lion rampant. No alcohol was sold in the stadium, but Aidan could see that many of the fans were drunk anyway.

The Eagles scored a goal, and the opposite side of the stadium erupted in cheers. As Aidan watched, a heavyset man in a wifebeater T-shirt stood up in the front row in Liam's section and yelled, "Bloody wankers!" waving his fist at the field.

"Sit the fuck down!" another man yelled from behind him.

The man in the wifebeater turned around and said, "I'll stand if I bloody well want to! And you can kiss my bloody arse if you don't like it!"

The men around the front row laughed and cheered, but the man behind said, "I wouldn't kiss your bloody arse because I don't know what's been shoved up it!"

His mates laughed and high-fived him. Aidan couldn't help smirking himself. But then he watched in horror as the man in the front reached down and grabbed a bottle from the floor, then turned around and heaved it at the man behind. "Shove that, you bloody poofter!" he yelled.

Liam moved in to quash the dispute, but he was too late. Friends of the man in back began throwing programs, bottles, and empty food containers at the men in front. In the middle of the melee, a skinny, tattooed Brit in an oversize Millwall T-shirt hurled an empty beer bottle down to the playing field, where he hit a Tunisian player square in the head.

Tunisians in the opposite stands began swarming down onto the field, aimed at the British, as Liam waded into the crowd in search of the bottle thrower. Aidan abandoned his staircase and pushed against the swarming British fans. He had to leap across a couple of rows of chairs toward Liam, who had disappeared in a sea of chaos.

"Liam! Where are you?" Aidan yelled, his adrenaline surging. Ahead of him, Liam rose from the bleachers, two supporters clinging to him. It was a majestic sight, seeing his tanned, toned body appearing like Hercules'.

The air smelled of spilled beer, sweat, and testosterone, and it excited Aidan in a way that almost frightened him. The roar of angry fans, yelling in English and Arabic, rose and fell, punctuated by the sound of breaking bottles and fists hitting flesh.

The police formed a line just behind the advertising banners, holding up shields against the debris and the onrushing supporters. Unfortunately the police keeping the British and Tunisian fans apart meant the Millwall supporters were confined to the stands, where they continued to slam into each other.

Aidan saw Liam shake off one of the British fans as easily as swatting a mosquito, but two more assailed him, and he began swinging his fists. Aidan knew then that things were serious. Liam avoided using brute force whenever possible, preferring to outthink or otherwise intimidate his opponents. He was a master fighter, though, his skills honed through years of SEAL training, and intellectually Aidan knew Liam could fight his way out of this trouble.

But his head wasn't ruling things as he jumped over the last row of chairs and waded into the fight. His partner, his lover, was in trouble, and Aidan couldn't stand by and wait to see how things shook out. He elbowed his way past two men throwing punches at each other, and used his head to butt the side of an older man with a shaved head who was trying to slam his fist into Liam.

With a roar, the man turned to face Aidan. He ducked, grabbed the man's sweatpants, and jerked them toward the ground. The man's rage turned to surprise as he stood bare-assed in the stands, his skinny dick hanging loose. Men around him began laughing, and he stumbled as he tried to pull his pants up. He lost his balance and fell into a seat.

Liam had another man in a Millwall jersey in a headlock, and the man was pummeling Liam's stomach. Sweat pouring from his forehead in the heat, Aidan reached for the man's waist, aiming for his belt buckle, but missed. Another man swung at him, and he had to turn and aim a kick at the man's groin. "Yaah!" he yelled as his foot made impact, and the man's mouth popped open and he howled in pain.

Aidan ducked a bottle of Celtia, a local beer, that went flying past, the pale liquid streaming in an arc that splattered a pair of brawlers just below where he stood. He jumped back into Liam's battle, finally managing to get his partner's attacker's belt unbuckled. He had the baggy jeans down before the man realized what had been done. He was wearing faded white briefs with a yellow stain at the pouch.

The man stopped punching Liam and grabbed for his pants. Liam released him from the headlock, slammed him in the abdomen with a roundhouse punch, and spun him away. Aidan stepped forward and turned so his back faced Liam's. Both of them crossed their arms and glared at the men around them.

He felt the heat from Liam's body against his own. Both of them were sweating, their faces and underarms slick with perspiration, but the hot, dry wind helped wick away some of the sweat.

The pantsing episodes had taken the fight out of the Millwall supporters; they were so busy laughing at the men who'd been embarrassed that they forgot to be angry. More police swarmed the stands, forming a cordon to empty the stadium row by row.

Aidan's heart continued to pound as the police ushered the Millwall supporters down the stairs. The man in sweatpants took a swing at Aidan as he passed, but Aidan anticipated the move and ducked, leaving the Brit swatting empty air. Aidan struggled to remain as impassive as Liam, resisting the urge to smirk or make a smart-assed comment.

The police took a couple of the rowdier men away in handcuffs, one of them continuing to shout racist epithets as he was pushed down the stairs. The stadium's loudspeakers repeated warnings in Arabic and heavily accented English as the sirocco continued to blow, surrounding them in a maelstrom of wind, sand, and the smell of beer and urine.

Aidan and Liam waited until their staircases had been cleared, then joined the cordon at the field's edge until the stadium had been emptied. By the time they left, the adrenaline surge Aidan had felt when the riots began had dissipated, and he was exhausted. "You just can't keep your hands off other guys' pants, can you?" Liam asked with a smile as they waited for a chartered bus to take them back to the city center.

"It worked, didn't it?"

"Yes, it did." Liam flexed his arms and stretched his back, and groaned.

Aidan stretched too. Though he hadn't strained any muscles, he was bone tired. The hot wind had dried most of his sweat, and he was very thirsty. "And you always tell me that we each have to play to our strengths. I'm never going to win a fistfight, so I have to outthink my opponent."

"I wouldn't call pulling a guy's pants down outthinking him," Liam said.

"But it's an unexpected move, right? Straight guys don't want to touch other men down there."

An old airport van pulled up, and they got on in a crowd of police and additional security. They both grabbed a pole halfway to the back and stood there, rocking with the motion of the bus, as they returned to the city center.

Neither of them spoke on the long ride. Aidan struggled to remain upright; his muscles ached and his hair was stuck to his head with dried sweat. He just wanted to get home, to their courtyard shower, and wash away the sand and the stink in a rain of hot water. He yawned a couple of times and was grateful when the bus pulled up at the central station, a few blocks from their house.

"I'm getting too old for this kind of work," Liam said and groaned as he stepped down from the bus.

Aidan laughed. "You're only thirty-six."

"Today I feel seventy-six." Liam flexed his back and rotated his head.

"I'll give you a back rub when we get home. You'll be good as new."

In his past life, teaching in Philadelphia and living with his ex-partner, Aidan had taken courses in massage, gourmet cooking, flower arranging, and a host of other skills, most of which proved useless in Tunis. The massage lessons, however, had been invaluable.

Hayam, their brown, mixed-breed dog, was waiting to greet them at the front door of the little stucco house they shared behind the Bar Mamounia. She jumped up and placed her forelegs on Liam's knee. He reached down to pet her, then groaned again.

"Shower first, then bedroom," Aidan said.

"I love it when you get bossy." Liam walked out to the courtyard. A wooden tub on the roof of the house collected rainwater, which was warmed by the glaring Tunisian sun. A pump on the roof channeled the water down a hose and into a shower stall. The tiled floor was slightly canted so that the water flowed into a drain that led out to the street.

By the time Aidan joined him, carrying a big square cake of lavender soap, the water was already warm and Liam had rinsed off the sweat and sand. Aidan stood under the showerhead for a moment himself, letting the water cascade over his head, then opened his eyes and slicked back his hair.

Aidan lathered up and began scrubbing Liam's back, massaging the trapezius muscles just below Liam's shoulders. They were drawn tight, and it took strength and skill to get them to relax.

Aidan inhaled the lavender scent as he pressed his fingers against Liam's warm, bronzed skin, pushing against the tight muscles, then releasing them. Touching Liam's body was always a heady experience for him, and his dick stood at attention as he focused on the muscle groups beneath the skin. Liam groaned and twitched as Aidan found a tight tendon and massaged it into relaxation.

Liam stood with his legs straight, without locking the knees, the weight of his body resting equally on the heels and balls of his feet. He let his arms hang loose at his sides, so that Aidan could manipulate them with ease.

Aidan lifted Liam's right arm, hefted it, then let it loose again. He began working the biceps. "You get too tense out in the field."

"It's called being alert," Liam said. "You should try it sometime."

Aidan dug his knuckles into the tender spot just below Liam's shoulder, and the big man winced. "Watch your mouth, sailor," Aidan said, laughing. "Or there's a lot more where that came from."

He lathered his hands again and moved down Liam's back to the latissimus dorsi of Liam's sides. Those muscles weren't as tense, and Liam sighed with pleasure. "Man, that feels good."

"I know how to take care of you." Aidan squatted down and began rubbing the adductor muscles of one thigh, the sartorius and the quadriceps.

"You do indeed," Liam said.

Aidan could feel the precum oozing out of the tip of his dick as he ran his hands gently over Liam's massive thighs, skirting his balls and ass crack, giving the calves a quick rubdown. "Feet later," he said, standing up.

He pressed against Liam's back, his dick nestling in Liam's ass crack. He reached around Liam with the soap and began to lather his partner's stomach and chest. Liam took the soap and scrubbed his arms. Then he turned around, leaned down, and pressed his lips against Aidan's. Their dicks rubbed against each other as they shared breath.

"I should get tense and dirty more often," Liam said into Aidan's ear.

"As often as you want, baby," Aidan said, kissing Liam's neck.

Liam pulled away and gave Aidan a quick scrubbing. Then they shut the water off and wrapped themselves in big towels. Liam walked into the bedroom, pulled an old bedspread from the closet, and tossed it onto the king-size bed. Then he lay down on his stomach, sighing contentedly. Aidan was there a moment later, still naked himself, holding a bottle of massage oil.

He climbed onto the bed, settling on his knees with Liam's body beneath him, his semihard dick resting in the crack of Liam's ass. Aidan squeezed some oil into his hands and rubbed them together to warm it. Then he leaned down and placed his palms flat on Liam's shoulders.

"Oh," Liam sighed. "That feels good."

"Just you wait. You're going to feel awesome by the time I get done with you."

He continued the massage he'd begun in the shower, rubbing the oil into Liam's shoulders. The muscles had been loosened by the hot water, and they responded under his touch. He moved down Liam's body with ease and grace, coating Liam's skin with the oil. He paid particular attention this time around to Liam's ass crack, squeezing a dollop of oil directly onto the puckered hole and then massaging it in with first one, then two fingers.

"You're torturing me again," Liam moaned. "But I love it. Don't stop, baby."

The oil was a special blend Aidan bought in the souk in the old city of Tunis, formulated so that it could serve for both massage and lubrication, and he squeezed another few drops into his hand and oiled up his dick, which was still rock hard.

Balancing on his hands, he positioned himself behind Liam, pressing his dick against Liam's hole. Since moving to Tunis, he'd begun working out every morning with Liam, and though he still couldn't match the bigger man's strength or endurance, he was able to do a hundred push-ups at a time.

He began moving his body down and forward so that his dick slipped into Liam's waiting ass. His circumcised dick was an inch longer than Liam's but thinner, with a mushroom cap that pulsed an angry purple when it was fully engorged. Liam's dick was thicker and uncircumcised, with a fleshy cowl that Aidan loved to lick and suck.

"Oh yeah, give me your dick," Liam mumbled into the pillow, pressing his ass up off the bed in time with Aidan's thrusts.

"Yeah, you like that, don't you." Aidan panted, sliding his dick in and out of Liam's oil-slickened chute. He ramped up his pace, pulling out, then slamming in. As always, the emotion rose in him as they fucked; he could not believe how lucky he was to have found this man, so handsome, smart, and kind, who loved him and gave him such pleasure.

Liam growled and began humping the bedspread beneath him as Aidan whimpered with pleasure. He pulled his dick out and turned Liam onto his back. He slid down, rubbing his dick against Liam's stomach, his partner's dick against his own thigh.

He lowered his face to Liam's, and they kissed, lips against lips, tongue against tongue. Aidan could feel that Liam was as close to orgasm as he was. Both of them pressed together, rubbing and kissing until the smell of the lavender soap and the massage oil merged with the sharp tang of semen as Aidan ejaculated, followed almost immediately by Liam. The cum pooled on their skin as Aidan collapsed onto Liam, then rolled to his side.

The laptop on the bedside table buzzed with the receipt of an incoming e-mail, but neither man had the energy to reach for it and read the message. "It'll wait," Aidan said, snuggling into Liam's side. "Love you, sweetheart."

"Love you too, babe."

Within minutes they were both asleep.

Mme Abboud's Proposition

After a nap, another shower with Liam, a simple dinner, and a walk around the neighborhood with Hayam so she could sniff the messages left to her by other passing dogs and leave a few of her own, Aidan logged in to read his e-mail. He was surprised to see a message from Madame Habiba Abboud, BA.

Aidan had a complicated relationship with Madame Abboud. She ran the École Internationale de Tunis, which was not, as its name promised, an actual school, but merely a placement service for teachers and tutors. He had first come to Tunis in response to one of her online ads, only to discover the job he believed he'd gotten didn't exist at all.

He thought she was a deceitful woman who preyed on unsuspecting educators. But without her, he'd never have come to Tunis or met Liam, and so he'd maintained a relationship with her. She had hired him to substitute for instructors on vacation or out sick on a few occasions, when things were slow in the bodyguard business.

My dear Mr. Greene, she wrote. *I trust that this finds you well. I am working with a client who is in need of the unique services that you and your partner can provide. Could you please contact me at your earliest convenience?*

She concluded with a phone number. It was too late by then, but the next morning, Friday, he called Madame Abboud shortly after nine o'clock. "It is a most curious situation," she said. "I would like to speak about it with you in person. Could you and Mr. Liam come to my office?"

She was reluctant to go into details over the phone, she said. But it involved both a teaching and a security assignment.

Aidan was sufficiently intrigued to make an appointment for later that morning. When he hung up, he looked out to the courtyard, where he spotted Liam doing jumping jacks. He wore no shirt and only the skimpiest of nylon shorts, most likely putting on a show for Mohammed, the stocky, bald bartender at the Bar Mamounia, and any early morning customers.

Aidan shook his head. Liam was an exhibitionist; if he thought Aidan wouldn't mind, he'd probably be out there in the courtyard naked. But what the hell, he had the body to show off. From the French doors that led outside, Aidan watched Liam spring up and down, his strong calves bearing his weight as he slapped his hands together over his head in midjump, then brought his arms back to his sides.

Even though they'd made love twice the night before, Aidan's dick sprang to attention as Liam's muscles flexed and dripped with sweat in the morning sun. His internal count finished, Liam stopped jumping and dropped to the hard sand of the courtyard for a series of push-ups.

He could have been the star of a workout video; his form was perfect, his back stiff and his legs straight. After a dozen reps, he began clapping his hands together on the rise.

Aidan left him to his exercise and went back to the computer, where he tried to see what Madame Abboud could be up to. She maintained a Web site for her business, and the most prominent feature was an ad for a six-week intensive English language institute in Bizerte, on the northern coast of Tunisia. It was to begin on Monday, two days ahead.

Did she need a teacher for that program? But why would that involve Liam?

Though he had been living in Tunisia for a year by then, Aidan had never been to the country's northern coast. Tunisia stuck out like a thumb on the left hand of Africa, nestled against the Mediterranean on its north and east sides. He had been to the south several times, including a stint trekking through the desert on his first adventure with Liam, and to the resort island of Djerba as well.

He pulled out a map of the country. It was about an hour's drive from Tunis to Bizerte on the Cairo-Dakar Highway, but since he and Liam had no car, they would most likely take the train, which would take about an hour and a half. The geography of the area was interesting; there was a large lake just inland of the city, and a canal that led from it to an impressive harbor on the Mediterranean.

More research revealed that Bizerte was known as the oldest and most European city in Tunisia, founded around 1000 BC by Phoenicians from Tyre.

The harbor had been built by the French after they occupied Tunisia in 1880. France had held on to Bizerte, and its harbor, after granting Tunisia its independence in 1956, not surrendering it until after an uprising in 1963.

As he read, he heard Liam showering outside. A few minutes later, Liam appeared, his skin glistening with water and a towel wrapped around his waist. "Whatcha doing?" he asked, pulling off the towel to dry his hair.

The sight was enough to distract Aidan for a moment. "You ever been to Bizerte?" he asked when Liam had wrapped the towel around his waist once more.

"On the north coast? Long time ago. Why?"

"I spoke to Madame Abboud this morning. She wants to hire us for a job, and I think it's up there."

"I don't see why you keep working for her after she tricked you."

"It was as much my fault as hers. I did misunderstand her. And besides, we need the work. The phone isn't exactly ringing off the hook."

"We can get by." Liam started toward the bedroom, once again removing his towel.

"I want to hear what she has to say," Aidan said. "We have an appointment with her at eleven. Both of us."

Liam shrugged as he walked into the bedroom, which Aidan took for agreement. They didn't talk about Madame Abboud again until they were a few blocks from her office. "Just remember she can't be trusted," Liam said.

"I know. But I'm curious. Aren't you?"

"I don't get curious until someone starts paying me."

Madame Abboud's office was in the old city of Tunis, a few blocks from the Zitouna mosque. The rundown building's stucco walls were pitted and dirty, and the blue paint on the ornamental grillwork was still as faded as it had been a year ago, when Aidan first met Madame Abboud. Hopping over the cracked stone stoop, they climbed the narrow staircase up to the second floor.

"Very impressive," Liam muttered as Aidan led him to a wooden door where ÉCOLE INTERNATIONALE had been painted in a flowing, Arabic-style script.

"*Bonjour*! Bonjour!" Madame Abboud said as they walked in, jumping up from her dented metal desk piled haphazardly with papers. She was a small, dumpy lady in an American-style business suit that looked like black silk. "It is so good to see you again, Monsieur Greene." She took both his hands and, leaning up, kissed him on both cheeks.

"And you must be Monsieur Liam," she said. "I am sorry, but your last name is too difficult for my Tunisian tongue."

"A common problem," Liam said, submitting to kisses from her as well.

The drab room was brightened by posters of American sights: the Grand Canyon, the Statue of Liberty, and the Golden Gate Bridge. They sat down across from Madame Abboud in a pair of spindly metal chairs.

"I have a problem and I need your help," she said. "I am facilitating an intensive English course which begins on Monday, with many young people from prestigious backgrounds. One of them, sadly, has been threatened by someone who wishes money from his father. He needs to have security in order to attend the institute."

"Who is this person?" Liam asked.

"Will you take the job? I cannot share such information unless it is so."

"I'm not comfortable taking a job when I don't know who I'm going to be protecting or what the circumstances are." Liam crossed his arms in front of his chest.

Aidan watched the conversation with a small smile. He knew Liam wouldn't back down, especially given his distrust of Madame Abboud. But she looked equally determined. "Why don't you tell us something about this institute," Aidan said after the silence had grown uncomfortable.

Madame Abboud smiled and pulled a pair of brochures from the mess on her desk, handing one to each of them. "Six weeks intensive study of English," she said. "An excellent facility, on the Mediterranean coast. For many centuries it was a monastery, founded by St. Augustine of Hippo long ago. Bizerte was called Hippo Diarrhytus once, you see."

"St. Augustine, patron saint of brewers," Liam said, looking at the brochure.

Aidan stared at him.

"Catholic school upbringing," Liam said. "We had to pick a favorite saint and research him in sixth grade. I picked Saint Augustine."

"The nuns must have loved you," Aidan said.

"There are still monks there, but only very few," Madame Abboud said. "They organize retreats and rent facilities."

"Are the threats against the whole program, or just this one student?"

She sighed. "The boy's name is Maksat Bazarov. His father is very wealthy in their home country of Turkmenistan. Monsieur Bazarov says Maksat cannot come to the institute unless I can guarantee he will be protected."

"I understand that," Liam said. "But the threats? Specific?"

"Monsieur Bazarov does not say. Just that Maksat must be safe."

"How old is this boy?" Aidan asked.

Madame Abboud looked through some papers. "Seventeen." She looked up at them. "You will take the job? Monsieur Aidan, you can be a teacher with your excellent credentials. The institute offers courses in speaking, reading, and writing in English, preparing students for college. Monsieur Liam, you could be director of security."

"I'm not sure," Liam said.

"Monsieur Bazarov has authorized me to pay for your services on his behalf," she said. She named a figure that was significantly more than the two of them had earned so far that year.

"What do you think?" Liam asked Aidan.

"I'd like to teach again," he said. "Do you think you could manage the security part?"

"How many students?" Liam asked Madame Abboud.

"There are fifty. We prefer to remain small, to provide more individual attention."

Aidan glanced at the brochure. Students took an hour-long workshop each day in reading, as well as one in writing and one in speaking. There were two different levels, beginning and intermediate English. In the late afternoon and evening, they attended conversation groups, British and American movies, and other cultural activities to allow them to practice what they were learning.

"They all live at this monastery?" Liam asked.

"Yes. Meals served three times a day."

He turned to Aidan. "I'll do it if you will."

"Sign us up," Aidan said.

Madame Abboud beamed. While she printed out contracts for both of them, Liam said, "We'll want to meet Maksat's plane at the airport and drive him to Bizerte. And I'd like to talk to his father myself about any specific threats that have been made."

"Yes, yes, that is fine," Madame Abboud said. "I have his telephone. He will be happy to have such fine security guarding his son."

She pulled out the teaching schedule. "Can you teach advanced reading and advanced writing?" she asked Aidan.

He agreed, and she scheduled him for the first and third periods of the day. "Breakfast, then two sessions," she said. "Then lunch, one more class session, and then free time in the afternoon for local sightseeing and informal English conversation. Then dinner, and movies in the evening."

They signed the contracts. "We will say that your work begins immediately," Madame Abboud said. "Because I know you will both have much to prepare. So I will pay you today for your first week. Is that acceptable?"

They agreed, and she wrote them each checks. Normally all payment went to their business, which they owned jointly, but in this case they were each being employed individually. They took the checks and a copy of Maksat Bazarov's application, which included his father's contact information.

Once they were back on the street, Liam said, "Bank first. Let's make sure her checks clear before we get too involved."

"I think this is going to be fun," Aidan said. The sun was exceptionally bright, and both put on sunglasses. Aidan's were aviator-style, while Liam's had big circular lenses that reflected a kaleidoscope of colors.

"I wouldn't call it fun," Liam said. "I'd call it a job."

"Yes, but I haven't taught in a year. I'm looking forward to getting back in the classroom. And this is going to be an interesting challenge, since I don't know anything about the students or their backgrounds."

"As long as I don't have to sit in on these classes," Liam said, shuddering.

"You never know, you might have to. To keep tabs on the client." Aidan laughed at Liam's discomfort.

"That's not part of the deal," Liam said, opening the door of the bank.

An Unexpected Encounter

Liam expected the checks to bounce, figuring that would cancel the assignment. But they cleared, and he accepted the fact that he'd have to work for Madame Abboud, even if he didn't trust her. Back home he opened the front door of the little house, and Hayam trotted right past him, heading for the single palm tree in front.

"I'm going to dig out my old textbooks," Aidan said, walking toward the bedroom. "I have to put together a syllabus. Six weeks isn't a lot of time, and who knows what Madame Abboud considers an advanced student. I should have asked her if there are placement tests. And how do I know what the other instructors are doing?"

"Aidan, you're babbling," Liam said, but Aidan was already gone. Liam snapped his fingers for the dog, but she ignored him, sniffing around the base of the tree as if she was about to discover the secrets of the doggie world.

"Nobody pays attention to me around here," Liam said, sighing. He waited for the dog to do her business then trot back inside, right past him without even a sniff. "After you, Madame." He closed the door behind her.

He usually left the computer work up to Aidan, but Aidan was so busy, so excited to be teaching again that Liam opened the laptop himself and did some basic searching on Maksat Bazarov's father.

Nuryagdy Bazarov was quite the business leader, he learned within a few minutes. His company, Maximum Gaz, controlled at least twenty-five percent of the natural gas production and distribution in Turkmenistan. The country contained the fourth largest reserve of national gas within one nation's borders; however, it was landlocked, with limited means of transporting its vast resources to markets. The long Soviet occupation had stifled natural competition, and the country's arid deserts were largely uninhabited.

He looked around for his cell phone. He and Aidan shared a plan, though each had his own phone. "Aidan, where's my cell?" he called after hunting unsuccessfully through the living room and kitchen.

"Where did you leave it?" Aidan called.

"Not helpful."

"I'll call you."

Liam's ringtone sounded like a waterfall. Aidan complained that hearing it made him want to pee, but Liam liked it. He strained to hear the sound, which was very faint. "Where are you, phone?" he said.

Hayam looked up from her wicker basket, then buried her head under her paw.

"Hayam? Do you have Daddy's phone?" He dropped to the floor, but the ringing had stopped. "Aidan, call me again."

Sure enough, the sound was louder down there by the dog. Liam lifted her up, and the phone was there where she had been lying. "Bad dog," he said, putting her down on the floor and scooping up the phone. "You are not on our cell plan, so you can't make calls. Do you understand?"

Hayam sat up on her hind legs, her mouth open, her tongue lolling out, as if she was expecting a treat.

"Fine. Have it your way." He stood up, grabbed one of the bone-shaped treats from the canister on the kitchen counter, and fed it to the dog. "Watch my fingers," he said as she gobbled it greedily.

The phone was uncomfortably warm as he dialed the number from Maksat Bazarov's application form. A woman answered in what sounded a lot like Turkish. Liam knew some basic phrases in a number of languages, but his Turkish was pretty limited. "*Ingilizce?*" he asked.

"Yes, may I help you?" the woman replied.

"I'm trying to reach Nuryagdy Bazarov," he said and explained the circumstances.

"Mr. Bazarov is not in the office," she said. "But you are in Tunis?"

"Yes."

"He comes to Tunis tomorrow," she said. "You would like to speak with him then?"

"That would be great."

She put him on hold for a minute, and when she returned, she had the details of his flight arrival and departure. "He does not speak English much," she said.

"But his assistant is with him who can be his translator."

He made arrangements to meet the man at the airport restaurant the next morning at eleven, and hung up, satisfied with his progress. When he met Bazarov, he would find out when the boy was arriving in Tunis, and make plans to escort him to Bizerte.

Aidan was still immersed in his books and papers, so Liam walked across the courtyard to the Bar Mamounia for a glass of wine.

He had just ordered when Abdullah, a young Tunisian he knew, scampered up to him and kissed his neck, wrapping his arms around Liam's torso. "Liam!" he said. "You have come to see me!"

"No, Abdullah," Liam said, prying the boy's arms away. "I came in for a drink."

"But Aidan is not with you. He has left? Gone back to America?"

Liam laughed at the boy's hopeful face. "No, Abdullah, he's still here."

Abdullah crossed his arms and pouted. "Why can you no love me?"

"Because I love Aidan," Liam said gently. "Now be a good boy and go play with your friends." He shooed the Tunisian away.

Not that he wouldn't consider a quick roll in the sack with Abdullah. The boy had some definite talents, and Liam had availed himself of those in the past, before he met Aidan. But he was a good Catholic boy, after all, and he believed in monogamy, even if he doubted the principal of his Catholic school, Father

Bernard, would approve of who he was being monogamous with. Another man—and a Jew at that.

He smiled as he tipped the glass to his face. He'd come a long way from St. Mary and St. Peter Academy in New Brunswick, New Jersey. It had been a series of big jumps—from a sheltered Catholic school upbringing to boot camp at the Great Lakes Naval Training Center on the western shore of Lake Michigan, halfway between Chicago and Milwaukee. Though his father often swore, Liam had made a pledge in eighth grade never to curse himself. That pledge went out the barracks window during his first week.

He'd never been the brainiest kid, but his intellect shone in basic training. He was accustomed to all-male environments, but not the kind of closeness of men thrown together twenty-four hours a day. He had struggled to understand why his dick rose every time one of his bunkmates stripped down, and he channeled all his fear and confusion into a determination to succeed. Nobody could suspect him of being a faggot if he was the best sailor in the platoon.

He had memorized the eleven general orders for a sentry, the navy chain of command, and the navy core values before arriving at boot camp. He had a natural talent for weapons, and his marksmanship scores were the highest in his squad. He was a strong swimmer, had run cross-country in high school, and could go for long periods without sleep—especially if his father was drunk and rampaging around the house.

He had learned to drink in the navy. As a teenager, he'd been scared shitless of ending up an alcoholic like his father. But once he had mastered boot camp and settled into life as a sailor, he found he could have a couple of beers or share a bottle of wine without danger. Even at thirty-six, he was still careful about what he drank, how much, and when; there was no way he was ending up like his old man.

His father had been sure Liam would flunk out of basic training, but Liam had thrived in the military, eventually being accepted for SEAL training. That was another whole world shift, one that was almost as life changing.

He drained his wine and left a few dinars on the bar for Mohammed, then walked back across the courtyard to the house. "How do you feel about pizza?" Aidan asked. He was sitting at the kitchen table, with a stack of books and a pile of papers around him.

"In general? Or for dinner tonight?"

"I meant to go grocery shopping this afternoon, but I got distracted."

"I'll take Hayam and pick something up while we're out." Liam grabbed the dog's leash, setting her into paroxysms of jumping and slavering, and once he had her hooked up, they walked out. The sun was sinking below the horizon, and the muezzin at the Zitouna mosque was calling the faithful to evening prayer.

The old lady from next door was sweeping her front step, and he nodded to her and said, "*Salaam alaikum*," as they passed.

She glared at Hayam and only returned Liam's greeting when the dog had moved on to the next house.

He smiled and waited for Hayam to squat in a patch of brown grass and relieve her bladder. He liked Tunis, had found a home there, but thought there was still so much of the world to explore, he wasn't sure he'd stay in Tunis forever.

The SEALs had opened his eyes to the larger world. He had come to the navy with most of an associate's degree from a community college back in New Jersey, and he'd finished his remaining courses stationed at a base in Florida. Then he had shipped out to the Persian Gulf, where he had begun to study Arabic, just to pass the time, and that had helped when he applied to the SEALs.

In his years as a SEAL, he'd seen many of the more dangerous parts of the world, and he'd learned how to get by on his wits and his strength. He had discovered he could endure pain, sleeplessness, dehydration, and a host of other problems more easily than most men. He'd accepted the fact that he was considered handsome just as he accepted that he'd never be the most accomplished SEAL in the service, because there was always a small part of his brain that was focused on hiding his attraction to other men.

He crossed the street and turned the corner, to a takeout place run by a pair of Italian brothers. He ordered a large *quattro stagione* and said he'd be back to pick it up. The older of the two brothers handed him a piece of sausage for Hayam, who gobbled it greedily from his hands.

Leaving the café, he ran into a pair of French-speaking male tourists, laughing and chattering. One dropped to the ground to pet Hayam. *"Quel mignon!"* he said.

Liam knew just enough French to understand that was a compliment. He smiled, and the man who'd remained standing returned the smile wolfishly, licking his lips.

Liam shook his head slightly, pulled on Hayam's leash, and kept walking. That was not an interchange he'd share with Aidan.

He wondered what his life might have been like had he admitted to himself earlier that he was gay— maybe even before going into the navy. Where would he be? Still in New Brunswick? What else could he do besides be a soldier or a bodyguard?

His world had shifted again once he admitted to himself that he was gay, that he wanted to have sex with other men. He'd known then that he couldn't stay in the military, because he didn't want to make a life based on lying. He came out to his commanding officer soon after and accepted his discharge.

He directed Hayam down the street toward a grocery that had a salad bar, where he loaded up a big plastic container with lettuce, tomato, and a bunch of vegetables. Then to the wine bar, where he bought a bottle of the Vieux Magon he and Aidan liked.

Aidan. The ESL teacher from Philadelphia had been the cause of his most recent world shaking. After a brief stint back in New Jersey, Liam had grabbed a freelance job in Tunis, eventually setting himself up as a bodyguard. He'd had a few contacts and had been able to build a customer list and get referrals based on his abilities. Then he had met Aidan in the Bar

Mamounia, mistaking him for a potential client named Charles Carlucci, who wanted help meeting up with a Tuareg tribe out in the desert.

By then it was time to pick up the pizza. Carrying it home, he remembered that moment in the bar when he felt something shift inside him. It was something he hadn't felt before—an attraction that was more than sexual desire. The connection between them had brought Aidan into Liam's bed—where he had remained ever since. And, thought Liam, he couldn't be happier about the situation.

When he walked back into the house, Aidan was still at the kitchen table, with all his books and papers. "Where are we going to eat?" Liam asked.

"Sorry. I'll get this out of the way."

Liam dropped the pizza, the salad, and the wine on the counter and washed his hands while Aidan packed up his class materials.

"You really are excited about this assignment, aren't you?" Liam asked as they dug into the pizza.

"I am. I didn't realize how much I missed teaching."

"Think you might want to go back to it full-time?"

Aidan looked up from his slice. "And give up working with you? Not a chance."

Liam smiled. He had been worried that Aidan's enthusiasm for teaching might mean they wouldn't work together, and he realized with a start how intertwined they had become in the last year.

He was still thinking of that when they settled into bed together. Aidan knew his habits and tolerated his idiosyncrasies. Together they formed a partnership that was greater than the two of them, and Liam didn't want that to end. He reached his arm over Aidan and pulled him close. He kissed the back of Aidan's neck, and Aidan snuggled up against him.

"Love you, babe," Liam said.

"You too, sweetheart." Aidan yawned, and the two of them drifted off to sleep.

The next morning, Aidan went to see Madame Abboud again. Liam worked out, then donned his leather vest, cargo shorts, and sandals. It was his standard attire, particularly for meeting clients. He wanted to show off his muscles and appear almost barbarian. It was what a client wanted to see in a bodyguard, after all.

He took a city bus to the airport for his eleven o'clock meeting with Nuryagdy Bazarov. His cell phone rang as he was walking into the main terminal.

"I am Ullyanov," the man on the other end said, emphasizing the middle syllable. "Assistant to Mr. Bazarov. We are walking off plane now."

They met a few minutes later at a coffee shop just outside the baggage check. Bazarov was older than Liam expected, in his midfifties, with dark hair growing gray at the temples. He wore an elegant business suit in charcoal gray; Aidan probably would have recognized the designer. His assistant, Ullyanov, was a slim man in his late twenties, with owlish horn-rimmed glasses and a haircut that was almost military short.

There was a teenager with them. Ullyanov introduced himself, Bazarov, and the young man. "This is Maksat."

The boy stood there sullenly, not accepting Liam's outstretched hand.

Liam looked down at his hand, then at the boy, who glared at him. "I guess you prefer a more friendly greeting than a handshake," he said, and he reached both arms around the boy, surprising him with a bear hug. "You need to know I will be in charge of you," he whispered in the boy's ear, then released him.

Maksat looked stunned, his father surprised. Ullyanov barely concealed a grin.

Liam led them to a table, where they sat down and ordered cappuccinos. Maksat held himself back from the table, his arms crossed over his chest.

So you want to be tough, Liam thought. Good. Just remember who's on your side. To Bazarov, he said, "Can you tell me what kind of threats you have received?"

Ullyanov translated, and then Bazarov spoke in the Turkmen language. It was a pattern they would carry out for the rest of the conversation, though Liam thought Bazarov understood more English than he was willing to let on. It was a smart move if Bazarov did speak English, because it could give him extra time to think about what he wanted to say.

"Maksat is a young man of very strong opinions," Ullyanov said. "He cares very much about his country and its political situation."

Looking at the boy, Liam wasn't sure. He looked like any ordinary teenager.

"His schoolteacher was a member of the opposition to the government. He often spoke to students about his positions. Then one day he was arrested at a demonstration."

Liam nodded, keeping his eyes on Maksat. The boy showed no recognition that this story was about him at all.

"Maksat, he organized students at school to protest this arrest."

"What did you do?" Liam asked, turning to Maksat.

The boy shrugged. "Friends and I go to capital with signs. We ask to speak to teacher. Police come and make us go away."

He looked back down at the table as if that was all there was to the story.

Bazarov began speaking heatedly to Ullyanov, who listened, nodding. "Mr. Bazarov wants you to understand that Maksat is being very humble. He was the leader of this group, and our government makes note of that."

"And have there been threats made against Maksat? Kidnapping? Death?"

He could tell Bazarov understood that last word and that he cared for his son, from his involuntary shudder and the way he and the boy shared a glance.

Bazarov and Ullyanov conferred, and then Ullyanov said, "No specific threat. But Mr. Bazarov wants his son to be protected. Maksat wants to go to this program. Then he will go to college in the United States."

"Perhaps the boy should go to the States right now," Liam said. "He would be more secure there. And I'm sure there are English language programs he could attend."

Maksat did not like being called a boy; that was clear from the way he glared at Liam, who smiled back at him.

Ullyanov said, "Maksat will have his way."

Bazarov glared at his assistant, who translated hastily. "It is of course his father's decision," Ullyanov said. "Maksat must improve his English before he attends university in the fall. This program comes with high recommendations."

Liam understood all too well. Maksat was a spoiled kid. He had run across many of those in his bodyguard work. But he was confident that a little discipline, judiciously applied, would keep the young Bazarov in line.

Neither Bazarov nor Ullyanov could or would give any more specifics about the threats. When they had all finished their coffees, Bazarov stood. "Thank you for protect my son," he said in heavily accented English.

Liam stood and shook his hand. "I take my responsibilities very seriously. Maksat will be in good hands."

Ullyanov translated, and then Liam said, "Maksat's course begins Monday. I believe the students are supposed to arrive by tomorrow evening. My partner and I will pick him up tomorrow afternoon and accompany him to Bizerte on the train."

Bazarov spoke, and Ullyanov listened. "You have no car?" he asked Liam.

Liam shook his head.

"We will rent car for you to drive Maksat to Bizerte and use there," Ullyanov said. "It is important for you to have car in place if you have to leave quickly."

Interesting, Liam thought. What was Ullyanov anticipating? "I can do that," Liam said. "Where will you be staying tonight?"

"The Hotel Africa," Ullyanov said. "We go there now. You can rent car and take us, please?"

"Certainly." While Bazarov and Maksat retrieved their bags, Ullyanov accompanied Liam to the car rental counter, where Ullyanov rented an SUV, with Liam as driver.

"What can you tell me about Maksat without his father around?" Liam asked as they waited for the paperwork. The terminal was heavily air-conditioned, and he regretted not wearing a real shirt.

"He is a spoiled child," Ullyanov said. "Nothing more to say."

Liam eyed him, but Ullyanov only shrugged. "I work for Mr. Bazarov. I do not know much about his family." He said nothing more until the paperwork was finished and he thanked the clerk.

They met the Bazarovs outside the baggage claim, and Liam noted Ullyanov hopped out and piled the luggage in the back of the SUV while Bazarov and Maksat got in.

Liam tried to play tour guide on the trip into Tunis, but no one was interested, so he shut up and focused on driving. When they arrived at the hotel, Ullyanov asked, "What time will you leave tomorrow?"

"It's only an hour's drive to Bizerte," Liam said. "Let's say two o'clock?"

"Noon would be better," Ullyanov said. "Mr. Bazarov has a meeting tomorrow at lunch."

"Noon it is, then," Liam said. "You have my phone number. Call me if there are any changes."

"There will be no changes." Ullyanov closed the door of the SUV too hard and led father and son into the hotel lobby.

Meeting with a Monk

Liam called Aidan as he drove away from the Hotel Africa. "I met the client. And I have a car. I'm going to take a run up to Bizerte to check the place out."

"What's the client like?"

"Spoiled kid. I'll be back for dinner. I'll tell you everything then. Love you."

He could tell Aidan wanted to chat, but he didn't like talking on the phone as he drove if he didn't have to. His whole life was based on paying attention to his surroundings, and he couldn't do that if he was gossiping with Aidan.

Traffic was light on the Cairo-Dakar Highway, and as he drove, Liam considered the job ahead. With luck it would be an easy gig. Nobody would try anything, and the boy would be safe for the six weeks he was in the program. At the end of the course, he and Aidan would deliver him back to the airport in Tunis.

He was contemplating that satisfying conclusion when traffic came to a halt, and in the distance he saw flashing lights. He had passed the turn for Al-Aliyah a few kilometers back, and the Lac du Bizerte was off somewhere to the east. This land was arable, very different from the deserts to the south. Beyond a hedgerow to his left, there was cultivated land, some kind of forest to his right. Clouds were massed ahead, and he could smell the rain in the air.

Traffic crawled, and eventually he saw the accident ahead. A passenger sedan had run afoul of a tractor trailer, and a lone patrolman in traditional bright blue shirt and white cap was channeling vehicles into a single lane. Liam's first instinct was to look for the cause of the crash. Had the car been trying to pass the truck? Had the trailer jackknifed on the road, tumbling over onto the sedan? Did it look like any other cars had been involved?

From the position of the vehicles, he deduced that the sedan had been trying to pass the truck, skidded on a slick patch, and slewed around into the truck's lane. There were skid marks on the pavement behind the truck, meaning the driver had tried to stop but failed.

What would he do in such a situation? And what would he do if he had the client with him in the car and they were stuck in traffic like this?

His mind worked through a series of scenarios until he passed the accident. Soon after, an industrial complex rose up on the left, and to the right he could see glimpses of the Mediterranean. He passed through the town of Houach Zarzouna—its two minarets towering over a cluster of single-story buildings—and then crossed the bridge into Bizerte.

Big tankers were moored against the far shore, and a tug navigated the calm, blue canal below him. Ahead he saw a cluster of eight- and ten-story apartment buildings painted in shades of tan and white, the square tower of the El Fath mosque, and the tall monument to the martyrs. This town had been the last part of Tunisia the French gave up, and as a former soldier he always connected to the sites of battles.

As he entered the town, it began to pour, torrents of water sweeping across the road, the palm trees shaking their fronds in anger. He slowed down with the traffic, keeping a close eye on the vehicles around him. Even without a client on board, it was good practice.

The deluge ended as suddenly as it had begun as he turned onto the Boulevard Habib Bourguiba. It seemed that there was a street named after Bourguiba, Tunisia's first president, in every city in the country— at least every one he'd visited. He followed it past Dar El Hout, the oceanographic museum, as it turned to parallel the Mediterranean coast. A few kilometers farther a sign announced the monastery of St. Augustine.

It was open for tours every weekday from two to four, he noticed with dismay. From what he remembered of Aidan's schedule, that was just the time that the students were out of class. If he were planning any kind of attack on Maksat, that's when he would act.

He parked in the paved forecourt of the monastery, but before he went inside, he walked around the property. The old monks had been smart and concerned for their safety; there was a stone wall around the perimeter of the compound.

From the outside, it looked like there were several buildings behind the walls, of one and two stories. There was a gate in the stone wall at the rear of the property, where it abutted a stretch of deserted beach, and another smaller gate in the side wall. The lock on it was rusted, though, and a creeping vine had snaked its way across the wooden door.

He was sweating lightly, despite the breeze off the Mediterranean, as he finished his circuit of the compound and walked up to the tall, arched front door. It was locked, so he rang the bell.

An elderly man in a dark brown tunic opened the door. "*Fermé*," he said. In French he directed Liam to return at two o'clock.

Liam's French was limited, so he launched into Arabic, explaining he was on the staff of the institute that would begin the next day. Could he come in and look around?

The monk nodded and stepped back. His name was Father Antoine, he said, replying in Arabic. "I am the abbot. Come in. Your people are not to arrive until tomorrow?"

"That's true. I'm in charge of security for the students, though."

The old man shook his nearly bald head. "Such a world. Security for school children."

He walked Liam first to the dormitory. The five resident monks lived in cells on the first floor. The second floor had been modernized, with communal bathrooms and windows that looked out at the Mediterranean. "Students will stay up here?" Liam asked.

"Yes, and the staff as well," Father Antoine said.

They descended the stone stairs and crossed the courtyard to a single-story building that contained five classrooms, each with chairs, desks, and a chalkboard. The large dining hall, used for assemblies as well as meals, was in a third building, with arched ceilings and decorated with ancient paintings of saints and miracles. The chapel was attached to it.

Liam was pleased. It was a fairly secure facility, except for the tourist visits. "Do many people come to tour?"

The monk shrugged. "Some days a few, some days none. This is why we rent out rooms to groups. We must support ourselves, you see."

Father Antoine introduced him to the brother who kept up the buildings and the one who maintained the grounds. Both supervised several Tunisian assistants, including maids and kitchen help who assisted when there was a group in residence. Another monk ran the kitchen, while the last was nearly ninety, blind, and crippled; he remained in his cell except for prayers.

"You see we are a small community," Father Antoine said.

Liam took some pictures with the camera in his cell phone, then thanked Father Antoine and promised to return the next day. He spent some time driving around the area, familiarizing himself with the access routes to the monastery.

The corniche along the Mediterranean was beautiful but isolated, great for an ambush. New-looking vacation villas behind high gates were sprinkled along the road, interspersed with a few local shops and a gas station. He stopped occasionally and took pictures, evaluating possible threats.

Then he returned to Bizerte. The city was a mix of modern apartment towers and traditional Arab architecture, curved archways and crenellated roofs side by side with plain concrete. Parts of the city reminded him of Venice, the way buildings were crammed close together next to the canal. However, these buildings were almost aggressively plain, their only ornamentation a series of doors or grilled windows. They were painted in pale shades of blue and tan, and often strings of laundry stretched from one window to the next.

He spent some time walking around the marina, noting the liveaboards, the ramshackle trawlers, and the sleek rental speedboats. He saw the chain-link fence and the security cameras even as he noted ways to avoid both. Liam didn't like coastal communities much; there were too many opportunities to slip in unnoticed. Water borders were just too damned porous, as immigration and drug authorities had long since recognized in places like Florida and California. As a SEAL, he'd often taken advantage of unguarded coastline to enter forbidden territory. He could swim as well as he could run, even loaded down with scuba gear, explosives, or other matériel.

When he had told Liam he had been to Bizerte once, long before, he was only telling half the truth. He hadn't visited as a tourist, or even a bodyguard. He'd been there on an op, one of many he'd participated in as a SEAL.

Sitting in the rented SUV at the marina, staring out at the restless waters of the Mediterranean, he remembered that trip and shook his head at the dangers he'd put himself through back then.

Missile Recon

Liam and his buddy Joey Sheridan were working out in the gym on their base in Sardinia when a noncom stuck his head in the door and said, "Hit the showers and then report to Colonel Hardwick in his office."

Liam let down the weights he'd been lifting with a clang. He and Joey both loped to the showers, shedding clothes as they ran. Both men were in excellent physical condition; Liam was taller than Joey by a couple of inches, but Joey was more muscular, particularly in his upper body. Running behind Joey, Liam couldn't help notice his buddy's tight ass and rippling lats and deltoids. But he quickly put those feelings aside, determined not to show wood in the showers.

He deliberately kept his back to Joey as they soaped and rinsed. "Any idea what's up?" he called across the shower.

"You been getting into trouble?"

"Not me. I'm pure as the driven snow. Must be you."

They finished quickly and trotted across to their barracks, where they dressed in their combat utility uniforms. Long-sleeved, button-down desert camo shirts in tan with mottling in various shades of brown, what was called the six-color chocolate chip pattern. The daytime pants were in a matching pattern, with four standard type pockets, two leg bellows type pockets, and reinforcement patches added at the knees and buttocks.

They reported to Hardwick's office. He was about forty, ten years older than Liam or Joey, with a trim build, close-cropped hair, and a no-nonsense attitude.

He stood up behind his desk and pointed at a map of North Africa. "Your destination is Bizerte-Sidi Ahmed Air Base west-southwest of the town of Bizerte in northern Tunisia," he said. "During the Africa campaign of World War II, it was used by Allied troops flying B-17 Flying Fortresses. Now, however, it's a Tunisian military installation. We've received intel that there may be strategic missiles there of Russian origin."

Hardwick put down his pointer and turned back to the two men. "Since Tunisia is a US ally, this is a touchy situation. Your mission is to infiltrate the base and search for such missiles. If you find them, you are to obtain photographic evidence, which could be used in diplomatic negotiations."

"Just photographs?" Joey asked.

"You are not, repeat not, to destroy said weapons if you find them," Hardwick said. "You deploy at twelve hundred hours on a flight to Tunis. You'll be met at the airport by embassy personnel, who will take you to Bizerte. Your contact will have detailed maps of the base and arrange to get you in the area. Carry some civilian clothes with you—I don't want you to leave any military footprint."

Liam always felt a zing of anticipation at the start of any operation. He accepted he was a bit of an adrenaline junkie. He got his rocks off by being the smartest, toughest, baddest SEAL he could be, and every time he went wheels up, he had the chance to excel once more. Failure? Not an option.

Nearly twelve hours later, they were in a small boat just off the Tunisian coast. He and Joey entered the cool water and swam ashore a few kilometers south of Bizerte's harbor.

He rose out of the ocean by moonlight, Joey by his side. They both stripped off their scuba gear, bundling it into their packs in quick, efficient motions. They dressed in their standard off-duty wear—jeans, T-shirts, and desert boots with thick socks. When he was finished, he waved a hand forward at Joey, who nodded.

They walked along the coast highway in the early hours before dawn. Except for their buzz-cut haircuts and military posture, they could have been taken for backpackers getting in some mileage before the desert sun rose. Just to be safe, however, when a truck passed, they hit the dirt until the coast was clear again.

They humped the nine kilometers to the base and, using aerial photographs, identified a section of the perimeter fence they could breach without being noticed. Liam carried wire cutters in his pack, and as Joey held the fence taut, Liam poised to cut an opening.

His hands were slippery with sweat, but he stilled his breathing, wiped his hands on his pants, and cut. There was no electric shock, and no alarms went off. Joey peeled the wires back as Liam stowed the cutters. They hid their bags just outside the fence and stepped through the opening.

There was too much moonlight for a covert op, Liam thought as they crept forward. Something didn't seem right; there was supposed to be enough cloud cover overhead to block the moon. He was about to say something to Joey when his friend grabbed his arm and motioned to the right. A single soldier in a modified golf cart was approaching, a rifle slung from his shoulder. The beam of his headlight illuminated the tarmac, and a small animal skittered across in front of him.

The cart stopped a few feet away from them. Liam focused on slowing his breathing, his back pressed so close to the building behind him it felt like part of his body. The soldier leaned forward, shone a flashlight that didn't quite reach where they stood, and then shrugged and drove away.

Their intel said the missiles were stored in a hangar on the west side of the base, and as they turned the corner of the building, they realized why the sky had seemed so bright. A pair of klieg lights were focused on the open door of the hangar. The golf cart was parked next to a truck, and the soldier who drove it was talking to an older man in a dress uniform.

A half dozen soldiers were loading missiles into the truck. It was too bright to use the night vision binoculars they had brought, and without amplification it was hard for them to discern the markings on the missiles. Liam pointed to himself and then toward the hangar. Joey nodded.

Liam crept forward, his digital camera in his hand. It was a high-tech model, but he had to get much closer to get quality images. He worked his way around a single-story building until he found a place where a drainpipe gave him some purchase on the walls. He climbed up as quickly and quietly as he could.

He had just reached the roof when he heard one of the soldiers shout a warning in Arabic. Immediately the klieg lights went out, as well as those inside the hangar.

Had he been spotted? If he was captured, it would be a big setback for US-Tunisian relations, and he knew the country was an important ally in the Arab world. His mouth went dry, and his heart raced as he lay down flat on the roof, trying to be as inconspicuous as possible.

If the soldiers came for him, Joey might be able to mount a distraction. Liam was poised for flight as his eyes adjusted to the dark. Then he realized that all the motion was away from him, rather than toward him.

He took a deep breath, then raised the night vision goggles to his face. Adjusting the focus, he saw the soldiers swarming into the hangar, the older man at the front door motioning them to hurry.

That was strange. If they had spotted him or Joey, why not come after them?

He got his answer a moment later when the night was shattered by the roar of a jet engine. A plane flew overhead, too low to be anything other than surveillance. From the markings, he could tell it belonged to the Tunisian Air Force.

What was going on? Why hide from their own surveillance? Was this some kind of rogue operation?

Once the plane had passed, the lights clicked on again. Liam was momentarily blinded, dropping the night vision goggles. As soon as he could focus, he brought the digital camera up to his face and began snapping shots. He zoomed in as close as he could on the missile markings, in Cyrillic, and on the face of the uniformed man in charge.

He stowed the camera when he heard three quick taps on the drainpipe. He turned around and crawled back to the corner of the roof. Joey stood at the foot of the pipe, his back to Liam and his gun up and pointed at the darkness. Liam paused for a moment, listening. He heard two soldiers talking in Arabic, too low and fast for him to understand. But he could tell they were getting closer to his position.

He swung around and dropped to the ground. Joey formed his hand into a gun, then tapped twice on his lower arm, and pointed back the way they had come.

Liam nodded. Two soldiers were tracking them, perhaps after finding the hole in the fence. They crept back the way they had come, not knowing any other way to get off the base. Twice patrols crossed their path, but each time they were able to blend against corrugated walls.

When they reached the building closest to the fence, they spotted a single soldier standing guard at the hole they'd cut. Joey tapped his own chest and pointed at the guard. Liam nodded. Joey took point, creeping up behind the sentry, then wrapping an arm around the man's throat, cutting off his air flow.

As Joey went through the fence and found their packs, Liam checked the soldier for a pulse. It was slow, but he was alive. Liam followed Joey through the fence and shouldered his pack. Out at the highway, they humped it to a twenty-four-hour gas station in sight of the entrance gate to the air base.

They slipped to the rear of the single-story prefab building, where a broken-down pickup rested on its axles, its engine and interior cannibalized for spare parts. They slung their packs into the back of the pickup and crawled beneath it.

Within a couple of minutes, a Tunisian air force truck came roaring out of the gate, soldiers hanging on to the sides carrying assault rifles. They stopped at the gas station, and a pair of soldiers jumped off the back, doing a quick survey of the property. Liam and Joey waited under the pickup as the soldiers tramped past, arguing with each other in Arabic. They sparred together all the way around the building. When they finished their circuit, they jumped back in the truck and called for the driver to move on.

Joey began to slither out from under the pickup, but Liam tapped on his arm. They waited. Ten minutes later, a second patrol passed, though this one didn't stop at the gas station.

"Ideas?" Joey whispered.

"We hitch a ride," Liam said.

They waited nearly two hours until a truck pulled into the gas station to refuel. While the driver was pumping his gas, they slipped around behind him and climbed into the back of the open truck, discovering a load of watermelons. They wedged themselves inside, and Liam pulled out his GPS tracker.

As the truck drove down the highway, he identified their route and the closest place to their access point where the driver would have to stop. He showed the display to Joey, who nodded.

Only the driver didn't bother to stop where Liam expected, roaring through a four-way stop without a look in either direction. While Liam went back to the GPS device, Joey grabbed a small melon and climbed forward in the truck. A thin black curtain separated the cargo area from the driver's seat, and Liam watched with amusement as Joey pushed aside the curtain and banged the driver on the head with the melon.

The driver slammed on the brakes, tossing Liam and Joey around with the cargo of melons, which smacked against them with the force of boulders. Stumbling and cursing, they scrambled over the melons and jumped out the back with their packs, then took off running as the driver jumped out of the cab and started yelling.

Liam laughed until the driver had gotten back in his truck and zoomed off. They found a path down to the ocean and jogged over the sand and rocks, until they found the cove where they had landed and reversed their process, pulling on their scuba gear.

They never learned anything more about the missiles, or who the man in charge was. That's the way it was in the military; you did what you were told to the best of your ability, and then you moved on.

He didn't take on that kind of assignment now, though. He insisted on a full briefing before taking on any job. Who was the client? What were the threats? Where were the points of vulnerability?

Was it because he was smarter now? Older and more careful? Or had he just given up on the military philosophy of following orders blindly? It was probably a combination of all three. As Heraclitus said, you can never step in the same stream twice—the river is not the same, and neither are you.

He had been changed when he fell in love with Aidan, that was for sure. He had always cared about his teammates; the military tenet of "no man left behind" was ingrained in his character. But he had always thought of himself and Joey, or any other soldier he operated with, as individuals working together for a common goal.

It wasn't like that with Aidan. They were a team—and he knew, deep in his soul, that if he had to, he would sacrifice himself to save Aidan. It wasn't even a conscious decision.

Even so, he would never share the story of the Bizerte operation with Aidan; he had never spoken much about any of the ops he'd participated in. That was part of the code. Even among his fellow SEALs, he had spoken only rarely of past missions, and usually only when something funny had happened. You just didn't talk about the dead, or the failures.

Thinking of Aidan reminded him that his partner was back in Tunis, and he knew it was time to get back there and see what Aidan had been able to dig up about Nuryagdy Bazarov and the reasons someone might have to kidnap or hurt his son.

Aidan Directs Traffic

While Liam was meeting the client and scoping out Bizerte, Aidan spent most of the day Saturday constructing syllabi for the classes he was going to teach. He was surprised at how his attitude had changed since moving to Tunis; he had been studying Arabic himself, and he had learned a lot about teaching from the materials he used.

He was still working on the laptop when Liam walked in. "What have you found on Bazarov?" he asked.

"Bazarov?" Aidan asked.

"You know, the client? Isn't that what you're working on?"

Aidan shook his head. "I've been figuring out what I'm going to teach. The institute starts tomorrow, remember?"

"And our primary job is protecting our client, Bazarov's son. So we need to be prepared. That's what I've been doing all day."

"You've been running around playing tourist. I've been working."

Liam walked behind Aidan and wrapped him in a hug, growling into Aidan's neck. "Forget the lesson plans and start working your Internet magic."

Aidan laughed at the tickling effect of Liam's breath on his neck. He squirmed under Liam's embrace. "When I finish what I'm doing."

"Now." Liam tightened his grip. "I'll make it worth your while later."

"Fine." Aidan saved his document and opened an Internet browser.

Liam let go and laughed. "Sex gets you every time. You are one horny bastard."

"It's not my fault you're so sexy," Aidan grumbled. "You think I like being led around by my dick?"

Liam reached into the refrigerator for a bottle of water. "Yeah, you do." He drank the bottle in one long gulp and then sighed. "Start with Bazarov's business. Let's see if he owes anybody money or has been dealing with anybody shady."

Aidan began combing newspapers and magazines for any mention of Nuryagdy Bazarov. They learned in quick succession that he was a Turkmen tycoon—one of the leading businessmen in his country—and that every one of his companies had the word "Maximum" in the title. In an interview with the *Financial Times*, he said that was because he lived his life to the maximum—and he expected the same dedication from everyone around him.

"He even named his son Maksat," Liam said. "Is this guy obsessed or what?"

"Or he loves his son so much that he names every business after him."

"You are such a romantic."

"No, look," Aidan said. "Maksat is seventeen, right? And Bazarov's first business was called Maximum Bina, and it was founded fifteen years ago."

"Could just be a coincidence."

"You taught me to look at what matters to the client. Maksat matters to Bazarov, which is what makes him a target."

"Fine. What does *bina* mean in Turkmen?"

"Do I look like the Noah Webster of Istanbul to you?" Aidan turned to the computer and pulled up a Turkmen-English dictionary compiled by Peace Corps volunteers. "It means building. Probably a real estate business."

They worked for an hour, creating a chart of Bazarov's business interests but finding nothing that looked shady. The most promising lead involved a natural gas pipeline that was to be built across the Caspian Sea to connect to one in Chechnya.

While Liam read, Aidan cleaned out the refrigerator, pulling together a dinner of rice and steamed vegetables, with a pair of chicken breasts he'd ducked out for earlier in the day. They ate at the kitchen table, both of them reading.

"We have to be at the Hotel Africa tomorrow at noon," Liam said as they were cleaning up. "So we can pack in the morning. Let's do some more research tonight."

Aidan returned to the laptop and logged in to a business database they subscribed to, which provided corporate profiles. "Looks like Bazarov has a net worth of about ten million US dollars," Aidan said, scanning the documents on the various Maximum businesses.

"It's not much, but it probably goes a long way in Turkmenistan."

"And this is just what we can find out about. There's probably more in offshore accounts."

"Let's hold off on doing any real snooping," Liam said. "We know that our client has money, and that he's received threats against his son. That's enough to start with."

"He wouldn't tell you where the threats came from?"

"They may not even be real." It was nearly nine o'clock by then. He stood up and stretched. "I'm going to pull together some hardware and then go to bed."

"What about that reward you promised me?" Aidan looked up as he shut the computer down. He smiled and licked his lips.

Liam laughed. "I should have known you wouldn't forget that."

"Hey, this may be our last chance for some privacy for six weeks. Didn't you tell me we're living in dorm rooms in this monastery?" He stood up and pulled his polo shirt over his head, then tossed it onto a kitchen chair.

"I'm sure you'll find us someplace private," Liam said. "You're good at that."

Aidan unbuckled his shorts and dropped them and his boxers to the floor. He stepped out of them, scooped them up, and dropped them on the chair with his shirt. "I'm good at a lot of things."

He was proud of his body as he stood naked before Liam. A year before, when he arrived in Tunis, he had been slim and in shape but not muscular. Since then he had often joined Liam in morning workouts, building his upper body strength and his endurance. He was still nowhere near as buff as Liam, who'd been working out for years, but he was bulking up.

Liam circled around Aidan as he stood there naked, at parade rest, his legs spread the regulation ten inches, his hands clasped behind his back. It was one of their little games—Aidan as a soldier, Liam as commanding officer.

Liam liked sex with Aidan best when he was fully clothed and Aidan was naked. It was a power trip, Aidan knew, but he didn't mind. He was happy to be the subservient one most of the time—he loved having his nipples tweaked, his cock sucked, his ass plowed. And he loved it even more because the man doing it was Liam.

"I suppose you'll do," Liam said, completing his circuit of Aidan's body. He reached one hand to each of Aidan's nipples and pressed his fingers closed. Then he made slight twisting movements that sent tremors through Aidan's body. Aidan leaned his head back and moaned softly, remaining in his stance.

Liam leaned his head down to Aidan's, and their lips met. Aidan tasted the tang of dinner's garlic aioli on Liam's lips, running his tongue over them as Liam opened wide. They French-kissed, their bodies still apart except for Liam's fingers on Aidan's nipples. Aidan shivered and squirmed as Liam increased the pressure, squeezing Aidan's nipples tight.

"Hold your position, soldier," Liam said, kissing his way down Aidan's chin to his throat. "Or else I'll have to punish you."

"Yes, sir."

Liam released Aidan's nipples, then wrapped his hands around Aidan's back and pulled him close. Liam's leather vest hung loose, so their chests pressed together, skin to skin. Aidan's head rested on Liam's shoulder, and he inhaled the rich scent of the leather and the faintest trace of the lemon cologne Liam had applied that morning.

Liam kissed his way down to Aidan's shoulder as his hands traveled over Aidan's buttocks, tracing the fine hairs there. Aidan shuddered when Liam's index finger penetrated him. "You're not holding your position," Liam said.

"Fuck that." Aidan raised his right leg and wrapped it around Liam's beefy thigh. "Or fuck me. Either one."

Liam released his grip and stepped back, pushing Aidan's leg away. "You need to know who's boss around here," he said, folding his arms over his broad chest.

"Yeah, yeah, yeah, you're in charge. You're the big stud. I know." He moved toward Liam, but the bigger man stepped back.

"Wrong answer. I'm going in to pack up those supplies. See you in the morning."

"Liam!" Aidan stood there, naked, his dick dripping precum, his heart racing. "You wouldn't."

"No?" Liam stood there stoic for a minute, then laughed. "No, I wouldn't."

He picked up Aidan and tossed him over his shoulder as lightly as if he were toting a fifty-pound bag of rice.

Aidan luxuriated in the feeling of closeness to Liam, of being totally controlled and protected by this big man. He rested his head against Liam's back, his cheek against smooth leather, his nostrils filling with the scent of the cowhide. He felt one of Liam's big hands pressed against his butt cheek. Aidan's stiff dick was jammed against Liam's chest, and his legs dangled, his feet banging against Liam's thighs as they walked into the bedroom.

Liam lay Aidan down on the bed on his back. "I love you so much that sometimes I think I could just look at you naked forever," Liam said, smiling.

Aidan arched his back with need, pressing his stiff dick upward. Liam took the hint, dropping to the bed and taking Aidan's dick in his mouth. "Oh my God," Aidan groaned.

Liam's mouth was so warm and wet, and seeing his military-cut head bobbing up and down was a complete turn-on. Liam licked his way up Aidan's shaft, then twirled his tongue around Aidan's piss slit. "You're just a big tease," Aidan panted. "Come on, Liam, suck me."

Liam looked up from his work. "Are you going to behave?"

"Anything. Anything you want."

"Since you put it that way." Liam went back down on Aidan, taking his dick in all the way to the root, then suctioning as he pulled up. Down and up, down and up. Aidan was sweating and shivering and moaning as the force of his orgasm built.

Liam grabbed his butt, lifting him off the bed, and stuck his index finger up Aidan's chute once more. That was it; Aidan cried out and spasmed as the cum flowed out of his dick and down Liam's throat.

Liam reared back and licked his lips. "I'm going to do that packing now."

Aidan knew not to complain. Liam didn't have the same level of desire he did; he was good with sex once, maybe twice a week, while Aidan could never seem to get enough of his handsome, sexy lover. He sagged back against the pillows, feeling completely spent, and was sound asleep before Liam joined him in bed.

The next morning was a crazy rush, packing and organizing. Aidan made sure there was enough food for Hayam, and that Mohammed, the bartender would let her out regularly.

Around eleven thirty, they packed the last bags and coolers into the rented SUV, and Aidan drove them to the Hotel Africa. Liam dialed Ullyanov's cell phone and made arrangements to pick up Maksat at the valet station.

"You never did tell me anything about this kid," Aidan said when Liam had finished.

"Handsome and spoiled."

"Handsome how?"

"Aidan. He's seventeen."

"So? I'm not going to fuck him. Just look at him."

"You can be a real pig sometimes, you know that?"

Aidan laughed. "I'm just not as repressed as you are. I can appreciate a good-looking guy without wanting his dick in my mouth."

"There's the hotel. Don't say anything like that in front of the client."

Aidan bit back a retort and pulled up in front of a uniformed doorman. Liam hopped out of the car and returned a moment later carrying a duffel bag on his shoulder, with a teenage boy and two older men following him.

The boy was handsome, Aidan agreed. Dark, wavy hair hung to his shoulders, and his eyes were black and smoldering. Just the faintest hint of a beard colored his chin. He was about six feet tall, slim, with a graceful carriage. Even at a glance, Aidan could tell his clothes were expensive, something stylish from London or Milan.

He got out of the SUV and helped Liam load the duffel and a small backpack. Liam introduced them, and then the boy climbed in the backseat and closed the door.

Bazarov said something in Turkmen to Ullyanov, who said, "Mr. Bazarov says you will take care of his son." It wasn't a request, more like an order.

"As if he was my own," Liam said.

Bazarov nodded, then turned and walked back into the hotel, followed by Ullyanov.

"We're on our way, then." Aidan climbed back into the driver's seat. As he was pulling out into the traffic of the Avenue Habib Bourguiba, he said, "How good is your English, Maksat?"

"You call me Maks," the boy said. "Is okay, my English."

"It'll be a lot better in six weeks," Aidan said cheerfully.

Liam directed them out of the city and onto the Cairo-Dakar Highway. It was a sunny day, and the streets were crowded with trucks, taxis, and every make and model of car. Aidan tried to make conversation with Maks, who answered in monosyllables. By the time they had passed the turnoff to Cebalat, Aidan was losing patience. "Do you want to improve your English, Maks?"

"I must, for go to college in US."

"Then talk to me," Aidan said. "The only way you improve a language is to use it. Speak it, read it, listen to it. Tell me something. Tell me about where you live in Turkmenistan."

In bits and pieces, Maks began to speak. By the time they arrived in Bizerte, Aidan knew Maks liked soccer, expensive sunglasses, and American hip-hop music. Maks's English improved as he got more comfortable, and Aidan was confident that by the end of the six weeks, he'd be speaking well enough to succeed in the US as a college freshman.

There was general chaos as they arrived at the monastery. Madame Abboud was in the courtyard checking off names. A line of cars and taxis waited to discharge passengers, and no one seemed to know where to go.

"This is insane," Liam said as they sat stalled in the monastery driveway.

"You both stay here." Aidan unhooked his seat belt. "I'm going to see if I can help."

He hiked up the driveway past parents, kids, and taxi drivers. "Bonjour, Madame," he said when he reached where she stood.

"Bonjour, Monsieur Greene." She turned from the parents she was speaking with and began fiddling through her papers.

"Excuse me, Madame," the father said in French. "If you can just tell us what room our son is in?"

Aidan spotted the room assignment sheet and took it from Madame Abboud's pile. "Permit me," he said in French. "Your son's name is?"

He began calling out names in his most commanding teacher voice and dispatching kids and parents to the proper rooms. Madame Abboud disappeared inside, and Aidan directed cars back down the driveway, making room. By the time Liam pulled up with the SUV, Aidan had a system down.

"It's interesting to see you boss other people around," Liam said, smiling, as he pulled Maks's duffel bag from the car.

"It's what I do best."

Liam leaned down to whisper in his ear. "Well, maybe not best."

Aidan felt himself blushing as he pulled away, smiling. "Maks is in room number eight, and you and I are sharing room number twenty-one."

"Good." Liam handed Maks his duffel and his other suitcase. "You heard that, Maks? Room eight. Don't leave the property without notifying one of us. We'll see you at dinner."

Maks stared at him. "How do my suitcase go to room?"

"Just like this," Liam said, hefting his own duffel onto his shoulder. "Come on, we'll walk together."

Maks looked around as if a personal valet was about to appear from behind the dining hall. But all around him were other students, some younger than he, some older, who were all carrying their bags themselves. He sighed deeply and picked up the duffel.

Over his bent back, Liam winked at Aidan, who turned to deal with the next arrivals.

Maks was back a few minutes later, just as Aidan had cleared the last car from the driveway. He wondered where Madame Abboud had gone, and what she was screwing up.

"There is mistake," Maks said. "Other boy in my room."

Aidan looked down at his list. "Yes. Room eight, Maksat Bazarov, Ricardo Gazzili."

"I have room myself."

"No, you don't," Aidan said. "There are only double rooms."

"I am calling my father." Maks turned away, pulling out his cell phone. As he did, though, he bumped into a very pretty young Arab girl, with dark and lustrous black hair down to her shoulders.

Maks blushed and mumbled something. "English, Maks," Aidan said. "Remember, we only speak English here for the next six weeks."

The girl smiled shyly at Maks, and he smiled back at her. "I am going to see classroom," she said to Maks. "You will come with?"

He nodded.

She said, "I am Ayesha," and threaded her hand around his arm and steered him the way she was going.

Aidan laughed and turned back to his checklist. Forty of the fifty students had already arrived. That was good. Another taxi pulled into the driveway, and he smiled. For almost the first time since arriving in Tunisia, he felt like he knew what he was doing. It was a good feeling, even if it didn't last.

The Head Table

By dinnertime the rest of the faculty and all the students but two had arrived. Aidan and Liam sat at the head table in the big dining room, with Father Antoine, Madame Abboud, and the other faculty members. The other monks, they were told, would eat in the kitchen with the cleaning and grounds staff.

Jennifer and Monica were both recent graduates of the master of arts program in teaching English as a second language at the University of Illinois. They were best friends, trying to spend a year or more traveling overseas and working as teachers when they could. Jennifer was the prettier of the two, with shoulder-length blonde hair and a brilliant smile. Monica was mousier, with dishwater blonde hair and sunburned cheeks. They were chatty and full of buzzwords about teaching—tool box, empowerment, and so on. Aidan thought they would be fun to hang around with.

The head table was on an elevated platform at one end of the room. "We only eat here on the first and last nights," Madame Abboud said as the server, a young Tunisian woman in a bootleg Abercrombie & Fitch T-shirt and slacks, poured wine. "For future meals, faculty will eat among the students, to promote conversation."

And police the use of English, Aidan thought. He looked out at the room, where the students sat on wooden benches at long, rectangular tables. It reminded him of the dining hall in the Harry Potter movies, only with an Arab touch. The windows were topped with curved arches, and the saints pictured in the stained glass windows were posed against desert scenes.

He spotted Maks sitting with his roommate, Ricardo; the pretty girl Maks had met in the courtyard, Ayesha; and a group of other boys and girls, all laughing and talking. They were the best-dressed group in the room, probably from the richest families. Aidan was interested to see how quickly they had gravitated toward each other. Among them, they wore enough Prada, Dolce & Gabbana, and Dior to stock a small specialty store.

The other students were an interesting mix. He knew from the information Madame Abboud had provided to all the faculty that the fifty students came from eighteen different countries, most of them in Africa or the Middle East. About sixty percent were female. Two girls wore the hijab, the Muslim head scarf that was not popular in Tunisia. The others dressed like teenagers everywhere, in jeans, T-shirts, and sneakers, though it was clear that they all knew their brand names.

Aidan ate his salad and looked around the head table at the other three members of the faculty. Rashid and Ismail were both Tunisians in their late twenties.

As Ismail passed the dressing to Madame Abboud, he reminded her that he would need to pray five times a day. "Yes, the schedule allows you," she said. "There are no classes during any of the prayers. Perhaps you and Rashid can volunteer to lead any students who wish to pray as well?"

"I am not so observant," Rashid said in an upper-class British accent. His skin was several shades darker than Ismail's, and his shirts were crisply starched.

"I will be happy to lead prayers," Ismail said. He spoke with a heavy Arabic accent and was fastidious about his meals, quizzing the server about each dish to make sure it was halal. Aidan noted Rashid's look of disdain every time Ismail spoke.

The final member of the faculty was a stout, red-faced Brit named Colin, who lived in Tunis and taught ESL at a private academy, as well as to individual students. He was in his fifties, and from the way he downed glass after glass of wine, Aidan had a feeling he would need watching.

But he wasn't in charge, he reminded himself. This was Madame Abboud's show. After the dinner plates had been cleared, she stepped to the podium.

She looked small and mild standing there, dwarfed by the height and drama of the dining room. "I am Madame Habiba Abboud, BA," she said. "I am the directrice of the École Internationale de Tunis, which sponsors this institute. I will now introduce your faculty."

She read a series of agonizingly long bios. Even though Aidan was interested in the qualifications of his colleagues, he still had to stifle a yawn. "Mr. Aidan Greene brings us an impressive pedigree," she said. "He holds a BA degree in English from the University of Pennsylvania, which you all will know is one of the colleges in the Ivy League, the most prestigious group of universities in the United States. He also received his master of science degree in teaching English to speakers of other languages there. This is also a most excellent program. He has taught at so many wonderful schools that a list of them would make your head spin!"

She went on to list them in agonizing detail. It was odd to hear his CV recited that way, even odder because he felt he had left all that behind when he decided to join Liam in his bodyguard business.

By the time she read Colin's credentials, Aidan's butt was starting to hurt from sitting for so long on the wooden bench. But Madame Abboud was not finished. "Now I would like to review our policies with you so there are no questions or disputes."

She ruffled through the stack of papers in her hands. For a while the only sound in the room was of papers being flapped, until someone began to giggle, and the laughter spread around the room.

Aidan noted that the trouble had begun at Maks's table. Great.

"May I help you, Madame Abboud?" Aidan said, standing up.

She handed him the pile of papers, and he quickly found the right one. "Let's begin with our English-only policy," he said to the crowd. His voice was loud and firm, and the laughter subsided. "All students must speak English in class and in public areas. We also encourage you to speak English with your friends and in private gatherings."

He looked up at the crowd. "How many of you have been studying English for five or more years?"

About half the students raised their hands. "And how many of you have studied for one year or less?"

A small group raised their hands. Aidan was interested to note that they were all at one table.

"We have a saying back in the United States," he said. "Each one teach one. We're going to keep reminding you of that over the next six weeks. Each of you has something to teach your classmates. But you can only do that if you speak English."

He turned to Madame Abboud. "Would you like to finish?"

"Yes, thank you." She read out the policies about class attendance, curfew, and behavior on excursions into town. "The beachfront is off limits during class hours," she said. "But you may swim or suntan during the afternoons when there are no activities."

There was general applause. Aidan was sure that one of the attractions of the institute was the beachfront location.

"We have a special treat for you this evening," Madame Abboud said. "We are showing a wonderful American movie about teaching English. It is called *Dead Poets Society*, and it stars Robin Williams. You will remember him from *Mork and Mindy*." She stuck her hand out, the fingers split down the middle, and said, "Nanoo nanoo."

The crowd erupted in laughter. "I guess *Mork and Mindy* is a lot more popular in the Arab world than I thought," Aidan whispered to Liam.

The students stood up and streamed out into the courtyard, where a monk directed them through the back gate to the beachfront. "I'm going to do a little surveillance," Liam said. "I'll see you back here later."

A large sheet had been hung on the side wall of the monastery, and the students and faculty settled into the sand to watch the movie. Aidan wished Liam was there next to him as the credits rolled. It was fun out there in the open air, the sand still warm from the day's sun, the surf providing a low additional soundtrack.

The students seemed to enjoy the movie, especially the parts about becoming free thinkers and seizing the day. Aidan worried that he was turning into an old grump when he agreed with the Latin teacher, who said, "Free thinkers at age seventeen? Funny."

Most of his students back in Philadelphia had been older, from their twenties and thirties up. They had immigrated to the US in search of better lives, and recognized that they needed to improve their English in order to succeed. It would be an interesting challenge for him to work with younger students.

Liam returned as the first student jumped up on a table in the classroom. "What did I miss?" he whispered.

"The whole movie," Aidan said. One by one, most of the rest of the class stood up on their desk and saluted Robin Williams. As the credits rolled, Aidan felt moved by the power of teachers. How many students had he helped as a teacher? How many times had he been told how much his work was appreciated? Why had he given all that up?

Liam rose to help shepherd the students back inside the monastery. Aidan remained there on the sand until he was the only one left.

The Back Door

Liam couldn't figure out what was going on with Aidan. He was normally so cheerful, yet after the movie he was moody and silent. Liam gave up trying to talk to him. "I'm going to go check the perimeter one last time before bed."

"Be careful," Aidan said. But Liam thought it sounded memorized, like Aidan didn't care.

Maybe this was a bad idea, he thought as he walked down the stone stairs to the first floor of the monastery. They didn't know who was after their client, or even if the threats were real. And being back in an academic environment was doing something strange to Aidan's head.

He heard a rustling noise and stopped. Probably just a mouse, but—there it was again, coming from a closet under the staircase. He crept forward, pulling his gun from his belt. He attached the bright light to the barrel, then opened the door and flipped the light on. "Freeze!"

The light blinded the boy and girl in the closet. The boy's hand was inside the girl's blouse. Both of them stared out at Liam with mouths agape.

"You should both be in bed by now," Liam said, turning off the light. "Your own beds."

The boy and girl, both still shell-shocked, scampered past him and up the stairs.

He shook his head. This was what he'd come to? Scaring kids trying to find a private place to make out? Not exactly bodyguard duty.

The big wooden front door was closed, a skeleton key on a long chain hanging next to it. Liam unlocked the door, then locked it again once he was outside, and pocketed the key. Hardly worth having a key like that; the lock could be picked by anybody with a screwdriver and some patience.

It was a cloudless night, with a thousand stars in the sky. Orion, the hunter, was right above him, immediately recognizable by the cluster of stars in his belt. He picked out Sirius, the Big Dipper, and the Pleiades as well. The three-quarter moon hung low over the Mediterranean as he rounded the corner of the monastery.

Ahead of him, a tall figure stood at the back door to the monastery. Who was it? A faculty member who'd gone for a walk after the movie? A student breaking curfew? Or a thief who had recognized the influx of a big crowd with tasty valuables?

He crept closer. The man at the door was no student; he was too old. Nor was he any of the brothers or the faculty members. Liam was about to raise his gun and light when a seashell cracked under his foot, and the man at the back door looked up. He caught sight of Liam and took off down the sand.

Liam could have chased him and perhaps caught him, though the sand was an unstable surface. And chances were the man was a common thief. Liam checked the gate; it was still locked, though it could use some reinforcement and a better lock.

He finished his circuit of the property, pleased there were no breaches in the wall. He circled back to the front gate, noting that the brothers had a single ancient station wagon, which was parked in the forecourt, next to the SUV he had rented in Tunis. Everyone else in the program had either arrived by taxi from the train station or been dropped off.

Just for fun, he pulled his Swiss army knife from his pocket and opened to the screwdriver blade. Inserting it in the front door lock, he twisted it, listening for connection with the tumblers. In under a minute, he had the door open.

That would have to change.

Inside he padded around the first floor, noting no irregularities, finally climbing to the second floor. He heard someone playing a Jay-Z song and saw a couple of lights coming from under closed doors, but that wasn't his problem.

By the time he got to their room, Aidan was asleep in one of the two single beds. He noted Aidan hadn't made any effort to push them together, and wondered about that. But he was too tired for any angst; he stripped down and slid between the fresh sheets.

The next morning he woke as morning light filled the room. Aidan was already awake, with a towel wrapped around his waist. "Good morning, sweetheart.

I'm going to take a shower," he said. "It's seven thirty, and I want to get downstairs for breakfast."

Liam sat up and yawned. "Where's the shower?"

"Down the hall. We're sharing with the girls, Colin, and the two Tunisians."

"What about Madame Abboud? Does she get an en-suite bathroom?"

"She left last night to go back to Tunis. She'll be back in a couple of days."

"So who's in charge?"

"Not clear. You and I are responsible for Maks and making sure he's safe. But I don't know who runs things with Madame Abboud away. Maybe the abbot?" He leaned over and kissed Liam. "I'm off."

Liam pulled on a pair of cargo shorts and deck shoes, and then considered whether to wear a T-shirt or his leather vest. The vest won, though he tied the laces over his bare chest for propriety's sake. He made it downstairs in time to get the last of the eggs and bacon the cook had put out in big chafing dishes.

As he was eating, he noticed several of the girls looking closely at him as they filed out of the refectory toward the classrooms. Maybe the leather vest had been a bad idea. As a bodyguard, he liked to look fierce and well built, because it made his adversaries think twice about taking him on. Of course, his body also gathered him sexual attention. Sometimes it seemed like every British secretary on vacation in Tunis wanted to make a little holiday nooky with him, and it was tiring to fight them off. Usually a quick smooch with Aidan did the trick.

But these teenage girls looked almost predatory, and he was sure that hormones were going to run rampant around this little closed community. He was going to have to be more discreet if he wanted to fade into the woodwork within the institute, have the kids forget he was around.

He finished his breakfast and sought out Father Antoine. "I'd like to make some safety improvements around the monastery, if that's all right."

"That would be very good, but we have a limited budget for such things."

"Don't worry, I'll charge it all to Maks Bazarov's father."

The old monk smiled. "Then by all means, do what you need."

"I want to change the locks on the front and back doors. How many keys do you need?"

"Just the one will do," Father Antoine said. "We leave it hanging by the door in case anyone needs to go out."

"Not while we're here."

The old monk nodded. "Come into my office, please, before you go." He led Liam down a narrow corridor to a small room lined with books, with a simple wooden desk and several chairs. "Sit, please," he said, taking his own chair beneath an ornate wooden crucifix mounted on the wall.

Liam couldn't help remembering the principal's office at St. Mary and St. Peter's in New Brunswick. It was a similar room, spare and book lined, with uncomfortable chairs for recalcitrant students and their embarrassed parents. The crucifix over Father Bernard's desk wasn't as elaborate as the one over Father Antoine's, and the French-Tunisian monk was a lot slimmer than Liam's elementary school principal, who had so many jowls he was called Saint Bernard. The kids had joked that he had a whiskey barrel concealed beneath his chins.

But the feeling of reprimand was just the same. "Please tell me why you are here," Father Antoine said.

"I told you, Maks Bazarov's father hired us to make sure he's safe."

"But why? Has someone threatened to do the boy harm?"

"His father wouldn't say. But Mr. Bazarov is very wealthy, and that could make his son a target."

Father Antoine looked Liam up and down. Once again, Liam regretted wearing the vest that morning. It was Aidan's fault. If Aidan had hung around, he never would have let Liam leave the room dressed as he was. He could almost see himself in Father Antoine's eyes—but instead of a misbehaving little boy, he looked like a war-hardened soldier of fortune. No wonder the elderly monk was nervous.

"I promise you, Father, we don't know of any specific threat to Maks or to anyone here at the monastery. I think Mr. Bazarov is just a very nervous, doting father. He loves his son and wants to make sure he's safe."

Another trait Father Antoine and Father Bernard had in common was a laser eye. Liam felt the elderly monk looking at him, judging his statement. In this case, at least, he was telling the complete truth.

Not so when he was a kid. He had lied a lot back then, because his father was a drunk and his mother was too mild-mannered to confront him. Liam's sisters were five and six years older than he was, always flirting with boys and getting into trouble, and Liam had a rebellious streak that had caused him to act up in class. Instead of laying the blame on his family, though, Liam always said everything was fine at home and took whatever punishment Father Bernard meted out.

Father Antoine sighed deeply. "We will need one key for each of the monks, and perhaps you should have a key made for each one of the faculty as well. That way none of them will feel they are prisoners here."

"And the students?" Liam asked.

"They can feel however they like," Father Antoine said. "But none of them should go out of the property after dark without an adult."

Liam found a hardware store in Bizerte. He bought a couple of simple tools, some wood, and a pair of high-quality locks with enough extra keys. He spent the rest of the morning reinforcing the back door and replacing the ancient lock with a modern one. Though there was a cool breeze off the ocean, and the rear courtyard was shaded with a couple of palm trees, he worked up a sweat, and he would have preferred to strip down to complete the work, just to a jockstrap that would keep his private parts out of danger.

But that wasn't possible. He'd already raised a few eyebrows that morning with his leather vest. He'd have to suffer for the sake of propriety.

Aidan often teased him about being an exhibitionist. But he saw no reason to be ashamed of his body, and he loved the way sunlight felt against his smooth skin and the freedom of being naked, or nearly so.

He went back up to the room when he finished with the lock, hoping to find Aidan there, but his partner was nowhere in sight. He stripped down, wrapped a too-skimpy towel around his waist, and walked to the shower. The door to the room Rashid and Ismail shared was open, the dark-skinned Rashid lying on one of the twin beds reading. He looked up as Liam passed, and Liam nodded hello.

Their room looked like a college dorm. Each man had declared one side as his own, almost as if a line had been drawn down the center. Not like the room he shared with Aidan, where their stuff already spilled together, just as it did back home in Tunis.

He wanted to talk with Aidan, get his thoughts about the intruder last night and the issue of locks and keys. As he showered, he thought again about how easily Aidan had integrated their lives together. Even though Liam had lived in the house behind the Bar Mamounia for a few years before Aidan moved in, it had felt more like a temporary military camp than a home.

Aidan had hung paintings on the walls and loaded the cabinets with kitchenware. They shared most of their clothes, even though their bodies were different. Aidan liked his shirts loose, and Liam preferred them tight. They had the same waist size, and most of Liam's height was in his legs, so long pants were the only things they had of their own. And even those were similar.

By the time Liam left the shower, Rashid had gone down to lunch. Liam dressed quickly, pulling on a polo shirt and cargo shorts, and hurried downstairs, hoping to catch Aidan. But Aidan came out of his classroom mobbed by teenagers, and they clung around him in the buffet line. Aidan sat at one of the long tables with the kids. At least, Liam noted, Maks Bazarov was among them.

Liam didn't like the forced camaraderie of the dining hall or struggling to make English conversation with a bunch of teenagers. He spoke fluent Arabic, after all; why not just talk to them in their own language? But that would be breaking Madame Abboud's rule.

He still didn't trust the dumpy woman. She'd screwed Aidan over in the past, and in Liam's book, that made her someone to watch out for. And Nuryagdy Bazarov might be paying the bill, but Habiba Abboud was still in charge, even though she'd retreated to Tunis. He walked up to the end of the food line and peered ahead. "Do you know what we're having?" he asked the girl in front of him, whose head was haloed by unruly blonde curls.

She began to speak in Arabic and then interrupted herself with an embarrassed giggle. "It is pasta," she said. "I do not know the right name."

He leaned close to her and whispered, "Don't worry, I'd rather speak Arabic too."

She laughed. He made conversation with her and her friends as they waited for their turn at vats of curly pasta in tomato sauce and a huge bowl of salad, and then sat with them. He was flattered by the attention they paid him, even though he knew it was because he was an adult, because he was a man, because he had more muscles than all the teenage boys in the place combined.

Maybe it wouldn't be so bad there after all.

Together or Apart

When he finished eating, Liam checked the schedule posted in the hallway outside the classrooms. Mr. Greene was teaching Level II writing from 1:00 to 2:15. That meant they'd have to wait to talk until after the class was over. He went back outside the monastery and walked around the entire property, taking notes on security risks.

He drew a map of the exterior, noting a few loose stones on the ocean side, and a couple of places where the sand was unstable. When he finished, he waited outside Aidan's classroom as the kids filed out.

The pretty girl, Ayesha, walked out next to Maks. "We go swim today?" she asked Maks.

"I don't wish to," Maks said. "I want go shopping in Bizerte. We call cab; you go with me."

"I think you should stay around the monastery for a few days, Maks," Liam said. "Until we know what's going on."

"I am not prisoner. I want go shopping."

Ayesha twined her arm in Maks's. "Please, Maks. Come swim with me."

Liam faced him, his arms crossed. Maks relented. "Fine. We go to beach."

Aidan came out of the classroom as Maks and Ayesha walked away, and Liam gave him a quick recap.

"I'm sure he'd be okay on his own for a couple of hours," Aidan said.

"That's not the way it works, Aidan. You know that. We're hired to protect Maks, so we've got to know where he is and what he's doing at all times."

"That's going to be tough with a spoiled teenager."

"Tough is our business."

"Speaking of which," Aidan said. "I saw you in your vest this morning. Don't you think that's a little much?"

"Yeah, yeah, I already got that from Father Antoine."

Aidan burst out laughing. "So you're taking fashion tips from a monk now?"

Liam couldn't help smiling himself. "How do you think I'd look with a tonsure? Sexy?"

"Please," Aidan said. "So what are you going to do this afternoon?"

"I guess I'm going to the beach."

"I have all these diagnostic essays to read." Aidan held out a pile of blue booklets. "I'm going to sit at the beach with a clipboard and a red pen. I can keep an eye on Maks."

Aidan looked happy, and Liam couldn't understand why. "Diagnostic? You're a doctor now?"

"It's what you call it when you have students write something on the first day, nitwit," Aidan said.

"So you can diagnose their problems with English and then you know what level they're on."

"Sounds boring."

"Boring is my business."

"I'm glad it's not mine." Liam pulled the map out of the back pocket of his cargo shorts. "I started making a map of any security issues on the property."

Aidan peered over his shoulder.

"I'm going to replace the lock on the front door and patch up the mortar work here and here," Liam said, pointing. "And I want to do some more exploring, get to know all the little hidey holes."

"Have fun. I'll see you upstairs before dinner."

Liam changed the lock on the front door and gave the keys for the monks to Father Antoine. He'd keep the ones for the faculty until someone asked. When he finished with the lock, he resumed prowling around the property and filling in details on his map. He sketched in the parking area in the forecourt, considering where to mount some high-intensity lights to illuminate anyone pulling up from the road. He shaded in the grassy area around the parking lot, and pressed harder to indicate the scrub around the outside of the monastery's walls, the palm and olive trees. One of the olives would need trimming; it would be too easy for a trained soldier, or even an amateur, to climb it and use it to vault over the wall and into the compound.

As he walked and sketched and considered, he worried about Aidan's lack of interest in the business of protecting Maks. He was so focused on teaching again, it was as if he'd lost sight of the real issue. And to look so happy about reading essays? Liam shuddered.

As he walked the perimeter of the property again and again, always noting new details, he kept coming back to thoughts of Aidan. He had become so accustomed to having Aidan there all the time, charming him, making him laugh, providing insights and making connections. Where was that guy? Aidan hadn't even pushed the beds together the night before. That was so unlike him.

The sun was casting long shadows across the forecourt when he went upstairs for his second shower of the day. He was drying himself off in the room when Aidan returned from grading. "These kids have so many problems; I don't know where to start," Aidan said, dropping the pages he'd carried on the desk by the window. He yawned and stretched. "What did you do this afternoon?"

"This afternoon? How about today? We've hardly talked all day."

He was surprised to hear that tone come out of his mouth. Usually Aidan was the dramatic one.

"Well, let's talk," Aidan said, flopping on the other twin bed.

"For starters, tell me why you didn't push the beds together last night."

"Huh?"

"There's something going on with you, Aidan. I don't know what it is, but you're acting weird."

Aidan opened his mouth to say something, then closed it again. He pulled his legs close to his chest and looked up at Liam, who wrapped the towel around his waist and leaned against the door.

"I didn't realize how much I missed teaching," Aidan said. "I'm not sure that being a bodyguard is the right thing for me."

Liam stood there, his mouth agape. "Where did this come from? You spend a couple of hours teaching and now you're ready to completely dismantle our lives?"

"No, no, I didn't mean that. I love you, you know that. I'm crazy about you. But let's face it, I'm a crappy bodyguard."

"You are not a crappy bodyguard. Think about all the things you've done in the last year. How much stronger you are, for one thing. You always had the brains to do a good job at anything, but now you can shoot a gun and disarm an opponent and…"

"And I can make a change in someone's life through teaching."

"Why can't you do both?"

"I'm going to try. We signed up for this job, and I'm going to see it through. But you have to remember I have obligations as an instructor here too."

Liam frowned. "What does that mean, in real terms?"

"It means your first priority is protecting Maks. I'm here to support you in anything you need. But I have to focus on teaching my classes, grading papers, and talking to students."

"I'm not accustomed to coming in second with you." Liam crossed his arms over his chest. Damn, he was sounding just like Aidan. Was this what happened when you were in a relationship? You became each other? He didn't like the way he was behaving, but he seemed powerless to change.

Aidan stood up and walked over to him. "You've got that wrong, sweetheart. You are my first priority, no matter what." He wrapped his arms around Liam and leaned up to kiss him.

Liam felt his dick rising, but resisted, backing his face away from Aidan's. "But what about the beds?"

"What do you mean?"

"We always sleep together. Why didn't you push the two beds together last night?"

"Oh. That."

"Yeah, that."

Aidan released his grip on Liam and stepped back. "I felt weird. I mean, we're the only people in this whole place who can have sex. What if one of the brothers, or the maids, comes in to clean and sees the beds together?"

"How can we be the only people here who can have sex?"

"Liam. They're monks. Celibate, remember? And the students are teenagers."

Liam laughed. "You think teenagers don't have sex? I found a pair of them making out in the closet under the stairs last night. And what about the other teachers? Nobody says they have to be celibate."

Aidan smiled. "You're right. I was being silly. Come on, you can help me push the beds together."

"We're due downstairs for dinner in a few minutes. Let's save the bed situation for later." He opened his arms. "But we do have time for a quick make-out session."

"Mmm," Aidan said, snuggling up against Liam's broad, naked chest, still damp from his shower. "Or maybe we'll just be late for dinner."

It felt so good to be in Aidan's embrace. He smelled of salt water, sweat, and the lemon soap they used. His chin was rough with five o'clock shadow, his lips chapped. Liam closed his eyes and kissed Aidan, their lips just brushing up against each other at first.

Liam inhaled deeply and sighed, then increased the pressure of the kiss. He wrapped his arms around Aidan's back and pulled him in tight. He parted his lips and snaked his tongue out, teasing Aidan's lips and then pressing into his mouth. Aidan's dick rose, forcing against his boxers and slacks, pushing into Liam's thigh.

Liam's dick swelled too, pressing against the rough cotton of the towel. His body tingled as he grasped Aidan's butt, bringing the two of them even closer. Aidan began kissing Liam's chin and his throat, and Liam arched his back and groaned with pleasure. "If you thought I would give up sex with you for six weeks, you were very wrong," Liam said into the top of Aidan's head.

Liam felt sweat drip down his brow and along the curve of his cheek. He reached down to Aidan's waist and hoisted up his polo shirt, snaking his hands over Aidan's waist. He loved feeling Aidan's hairy chest against his own smooth skin. "If you start up like that, we'll never get down to dinner," Aidan said.

"I don't need food when I have you to nibble on," Liam said, nipping at Aidan's throat.

"Hey, no vampire sex. And remember, dinner isn't just about eating. We're here to keep an eye on Maks."

"You're a party pooper, you know that?" Liam said, pulling back.

"Call me a party postponer."

"If you push those beds together later, I'll show you a party in your pants."

Aidan burst out laughing. "Comb your hair, you big goof. We don't need to walk into the dining room looking like we just made out."

"I've got an idea. Tomorrow you can teach the kids what a hickey is. I'll give you a big one right on your neck you can use for show-and-tell."

Aidan looked horrified, and Liam laughed. "I'd better get dressed, or we'll be late for dinner."

Furniture Malfunction

Aidan walked into the dining room just as the last students were filing in. The head table stood empty, and the other faculty had joined student tables. There was one seat at the table where Maks, Ayesha, Ricardo, and Carla sat with another girl.

He turned to Liam. "Let's trade off, so the kids with Maks get to know both of us. You sit with them, and I'll go across the room."

"You're the boss," Liam said.

"Only in my dreams," Aidan said. He sat with the group who spoke the least English, and over the course of the meal painstakingly drew each one out about his or her homeland and reasons for coming to the institute. By the time the meal was over and he walked to Liam's table, he was exhausted.

The kids at Liam's table were just getting up, and Aidan arrived as Ayesha said, "Thank you for sitting with us, Mr. Liam." Aidan couldn't help noticing the way she looked at Liam so adoringly. He wondered if sometimes he looked the same way.

The kids filed away, and Liam asked, "You feel like a walk? I hear the beach is beautiful by moonlight."

"Why is it that I feel you have more than romance on your mind?"

"Hey, we have stuff to talk about. Might as well do it out by the Mediterranean as well as up in our room. We'll save the room time for something more productive."

Aidan smiled. "Whatever you say, stud. I'm yours to command."

"That's Mr. Stud to you. But we'll deal with that later."

They walked through the back courtyard to the gate that led to the beach. It was open, and one of the monks sat in a chair beside it. They nodded their greetings and walked out to the beach, where several groups of kids had already staked out pieces of sand. Aidan and Liam turned west, walking until they were out of earshot.

"So how do you think things are shaping up?" Aidan asked. "From a security standpoint?"

"This place isn't as bad as it could be. I'm glad I got the locks changed, though. Tomorrow I'm going to put a couple of other small construction projects in motion."

"Bazarov is paying for all that?"

"Ullyanov told me I could spend whatever I needed. Bazarov wants his son to be safe."

"Don't you think there's something fishy about that?" Aidan asked. "I mean, there must be something pretty serious to those threats for Bazarov to spend so much."

"He's rich," Liam said, shrugging. "Rich people don't care about money. They just want what they want."

Aidan remembered his ex, Blake. He was well-off, but he was a penny-pincher. Even the smallest of purchases had to be scrutinized. "If you say so. You need anything from me?"

"Always." Liam reached over and took Aidan's hand. Looking straight ahead, he said, "Before I met you, I thought I'd probably be a lone wolf forever. Work on my own. Have some sex now and then but nothing, you know, permanent." He turned to look at Aidan. "Now I can't imagine going back to that."

"Oh, sweetheart, I'm not leaving you. I just like teaching."

"But what you said before. That you were a crappy bodyguard and you wanted to do something you were good at. You don't believe that, do you?"

"I've got a pretty high standard to measure myself against," Aidan said. "You've got to admit that. And I'm never going to be as good as you are. I just don't have it in me."

"But that doesn't mean we can't work together. We complement each other."

Aidan leaned over and kissed him. "We do a lot more than that for each other."

"Mmm," Liam said. "I like it when you do that."

They kissed again. Liam's mouth tasted like the chocolate cake they'd had for dessert. "We should go up to the room," Aidan said.

"You afraid of being discovered?"

"No, I'm afraid of scraping my dick against this rock or getting sand up my ass if we stay out here much longer. You know I don't have much self-control when it comes to you."

They walked back to the monastery. The monk at the door said that at nine o'clock he'd round up any kids who were still outside and shepherd them in, then close the door. He complimented Liam on the new lock.

As they walked inside, they passed Ayesha and two other girls, who all smiled and said good night. Aidan thought the way they fawned over Liam was amusing, though he hoped Liam wouldn't get even more of a swelled head than he already had. "You had a busy day," he said to Liam as they climbed the stairs. "Carpentry, locksmithing. Not to mention charming every girl in this place."

"It's a tough job, but somebody's got to do it."

Back upstairs, Liam helped Aidan push the two beds together. The room faced the Mediterranean, so there was a cool breeze coming in off the ocean. The temperature was just right—not hot enough for a fan or cool enough for a blanket.

"Where did we leave off?" Liam asked, pulling off his polo shirt.

Aidan was surprised that Liam was so quick to strip. Usually Liam preferred to stay clothed and somehow more in charge, at least halfway through any sex play. Aidan crossed the room, flipped off the overhead light, and then came up to Liam. He wrapped his arms around the big man's back. "I think we were here," he said, leaning up to kiss Liam's lips.

They kissed, opening their mouths to each other, their tongues dueling. "Yeah, I remember this," Liam groaned.

He began unbuttoning Aidan's shirt, leaning down as he did to kiss Aidan's chin, his throat, and his neck. Aidan felt his dick harden, struggling against the fabric of his boxers. Liam finished unbuttoning Aidan's shirt and slipped it off his shoulders. Then he unbuttoned his own shorts and dropped them to the floor, stepping out of his deck shoes as he did.

In the moonlight, Aidan luxuriated in the view of Liam's body. There was something about a guy in a jockstrap that always turned his crank, some leftover from obsessing over boys in the high school locker room. But the sight of *this* man in a jockstrap was so much more amazing than any other Aidan had ever seen, in person or in pictures.

Liam's chest was almost square, tanned to a golden brown, with a tiny gold ring in each of his dark, puckered nipples. His stomach was flat and his waist was narrow, stray pubic hairs climbing beyond the confines of the white cotton pouch. He had a bubble butt that Aidan loved to wrap his hands around, and his legs were like tree trunks, the musculature visible just under the skin, like a Michelangelo statue.

Pressing against the pouch, Liam's dick had swollen to its full hardness, and in a quick move, Liam skinned the jock down and stepped out of it. He cupped his dick in his hands and offered it to Aidan, who dropped to his knees and took it in his mouth.

Liam's dick was fatter than Aidan's, though a little shorter. Aidan licked it from bottom to top as

Liam groaned and put his hands on either side of Aidan's face. "Suck that cock," he said. "Suck it like you want it."

Aidan relaxed his throat and swallowed Liam down to the root. Liam pressed his head down, keeping him in place, as Aidan licked and sucked the dick in his mouth. When he felt himself getting short of breath, he forced his head up, took a deep breath, and then began sucking in earnest, moving his head up and down on Liam's dick.

"Yeah, you love that dick, don't you," Liam said.

Aidan stuck his right index finger into Liam's ass, which contracted around him. He felt Liam's dick swelling as the blood pulsed and the cum rose. "Aiyee," Liam howled as the force of his ejaculation struck him.

Aidan was laughing and trying to swallow Liam's cum at the same time. "The whole monastery heard that," he said, backing off. "Usually I'm the one who needs to keep his voice down."

"Let them hear it," Liam growled, pulling Aidan back up to his feet. "I'm marking my territory."

"I'm not a fireplug you need to pee on."

"You've got a fireplug all right. And I know just where I want it." He looked down at Aidan and smiled wolfishly. "Why are you still wearing your pants?"

That was a good question, Aidan thought, as he hurriedly unbuckled them. Liam wasn't usually so quick—they often spent a lot more time on foreplay. Not that he was complaining.

He dropped his pants and pushed his boxers down too. Liam lay down in the middle of the bed and grabbed his calves. He raised them above his head.

Then the twin beds split apart and he fell to the floor with a hard thump.

Aidan burst into laughter as Liam floundered in the debris of the bedcovers. "God, I love you," he said. He pushed the beds farther apart and got down on his knees. He spit into his hand and used the saliva and his precum to lubricate his dick. Liam pulled his ass cheeks apart again, and Aidan slammed his dick into his ass.

Liam groaned. "Yeah, you like that, don't you." Aidan grabbed Liam's thighs and began slamming his dick into his partner's ass. Both of them were moaning and sweating as the moonlight filled the room, and they heard the distant sound of the surf washing against the sandy shore.

Aidan's hands grew slippery with sweat, and his dick rubbed in and out of Liam's ass, exerting a pressure that primed his pump even more. He bit his lip to keep from whimpering too loud as he made one final slam into Liam's ass and felt the cum rise up from his balls and spurt through his slit.

He collapsed down onto Liam, their sweaty bodies mingling. Then he slid to Liam's side, pushing the beds even farther apart, and they cuddled together on the wooden floor. "I love you, sweetheart," he said, resting his head on Liam's broad, smooth chest.

"I love you too, babe." He leaned down and kissed Aidan's forehead.

Liam On The Job

There on the floor, Liam leaned back against a pillow, Aidan's head against his chest. He wrapped one arm around Aidan's shoulder and relished the slight scrape of his partner's five o'clock shadow against his own smooth skin.

Late in the night, they rose from the floor, pushed the beds together once more, and went to sleep. They overslept, rising just in time to grab some clothes and hurry down to breakfast. They sat together, with a group of students Liam didn't know. The kids were still enthusiastic after their first full day of classes, and Liam figured that was a good sign.

While Aidan went off to his first class, Liam put on a tank top, jockstrap, and shorts, then went down to the beach. He found a flat section of hard-packed sand and began his routine: a hundred push-ups, a hundred sit-ups, then a hundred jumping jacks. He took advantage of the Mediterranean to step into the shallow water and begin swimming.

He did the breaststroke out a hundred yards, then turned west and moved into the butterfly. After another hundred yards, he switched to the Australian crawl.

He had always been a good swimmer, but when he joined the SEALs, he had stepped his game up. He had been one of the best swimmers on his team, and he felt at home in the water. He was able to shut off his brain and become a machine. Before Aidan, there had always been too many things he didn't want to think about: his father's drinking, his fear of his own sexuality, his determination to succeed as a sailor and a SEAL.

Even now, when everything in his life had fallen into place, he still loved to swim. There was such a deep pleasure in the way his body worked, the way he could slide through the water just like an ocean creature.

Flipping over to the backstroke, he returned in the direction of the monastery. He couldn't swim as much as he liked in Tunis; he had a friend who worked at one of the big hotels, who let Liam swim there, but there was nothing like the ocean for a good workout. He finished up with the combat sidestroke, developed by the SEALs to be more efficient and reduce the swimmer's profile in the water.

By the time he finished, he was energized. He took a quick shower, then sought out Father Antoine to tell the monk about his plans for lights in the front courtyard. He gave Liam the name of an electrical company in Bizerte that could provide and install the lights. "This Mr. Bazarov, he is very concerned," Father Antoine said.

"His fear is good for the monastery," Liam said. "By the time I get done here, your buildings will be in very good shape."

"It is all the Lord's way," Father Antoine said.

Liam simply nodded and left the old monk in his office. He had given up on organized religion sometime in his teens, when he realized God wasn't going to do anything about his father's drinking or his own uncomfortable urges. He had been raised to believe it was a sin to touch yourself or to long for sexual contact outside marriage. And sex with another man? An abomination, or so the priests always said.

As he was driving into Bizerte, his cell phone rang. "Good morning," Ullyanov said. "The boy is well?"

"Yes, no problems."

Ullyanov said he had arranged a line of credit with a bank in Bizerte to pay Liam and Aidan and to cover any of their expenses. "Mr. Bazarov, he want you to know he is trusting you very much."

"We'll do our best." After the conversation was over, he wondered again what was going on. Was there a threat to Maks? He went to the bank and verified the line of credit, drawing out enough to pay the electrician a deposit, order the lights, and reimburse himself for what he'd already spent. Madame Abboud had given them their first week's salary, so he took only what he needed for purchases.

He realized he was missing lunch at the monastery, so he picked up a sandwich filled with tuna, hard-boiled egg, peppers, diced tomatoes and onions, dressed with olive oil and a touch of hot, spicy harissa sauce, and a bottle of mineral water. He pulled the SUV over near the marina and ate with a water view.

A large, fancy yacht was pulling out beyond the breakwater and into the Mediterranean. Rich people, he thought. Was Bazarov just indulging himself—or was he really scared about a threat to Maks? If there was something credible to worry about, why wasn't he or Ullyanov telling them?

By the time he finished buying what he needed, it was late afternoon, and he met up with Aidan in their room. "These kids need so much help," Aidan said, showing Liam how many marks he'd made on their papers. "Some of them can barely write a grammatical sentence in English. I don't see how I can get them where they need to be in six weeks."

"You'll do what you can." Liam was feeling better about their relationship after their moonlight walk and the subsequent sex. Things might work out fine, if there was no big threat to Maks Bazarov. Liam could work on the security at the monastery, Aidan could teach, and they'd get paid. It would be good all around.

The next morning, after his workout, Liam was down on his hands and knees in the chapel, shimmying behind the altar to discover a musty passageway that led back to the dining hall. He filled in details on his sketch of the whole property, indicating security risks. The electricians arrived to begin installing the lights, and he spent most of the day with them as they ran wires and upgraded the monastery's electrical systems.

Thursday, Liam fixed a couple of broken windows and showed the stonemason the places along the ocean wall that needed to be repointed. Aidan was busy with teaching, grading papers, and casual conversations with the kids and the rest of the faculty.

Liam was waiting for Aidan outside his classroom following the afternoon classes when Maks and Ayesha walked past. Maks asked his girlfriend, "We go into Bizerte today?"

"Sure," she said.

"What time do you want to go?" Liam said, walking up to them. "I'll give you a ride."

"You are not my father," Maks said. "I am adult."

Ayesha looked confused at the confrontation. "Is good we have ride," she said to Maks. "Otherwise we are taking bus."

"I have money for cab." Maks took Ayesha's arm and steered her down the hall.

"What was that about?" Aidan asked, coming out of the classroom loaded down with books and papers.

"Maks wants to go into Bizerte. I offered to drive him and his friends, and he got huffy."

"So what are you going to do? Follow them into town?"

"Guess so. You up for some surveillance?"

Aidan held up a sheaf of papers. "Grading."

"Okay. I'll take on Maks and his friends myself. I assume I can handle a bunch of teenagers."

"Don't be too sure. But be careful. Love you." Aidan leaned up and kissed Liam's cheek.

Feeling Aidan's lips against his skin made Liam tingle, and he smiled. "Love you too, babe. Don't let the grading get you down."

Liam left Aidan to his papers and went out to the forecourt where the SUV was parked. He drove down to the Cairo-Dakar Highway and slid the car behind a screen of trees, where he could watch the driveway.

About ten minutes later, a cab approached from the direction of Bizerte and pulled into the monastery's driveway. With his binoculars, Liam saw Maks, Ayesha, Ricardo, and a girl he didn't recognize get into the cab.

He let the cab get a few hundred meters ahead before he pulled out onto the highway, then followed it down the Avenue Habib Bourguiba and into the center of town. Coming alone was a bad idea, he thought. What was he going to do when the kids got out of the cab, and he was stuck trying to park the SUV? Once again it was Aidan's fault. Their first job, both of them, was to protect the client, not to teach him English.

The town was very European in a way, its streets lined with trees, with a lot of charm. The cab pulled up at the Place Siahedine Bouchoucha and the kids got out. The medina was coming back to life after the noon siesta, but fortunately Liam found a parking space a few hundred feet beyond where the kids left the cab, at the edge of a shaded square of homes and stores with pink tile roofs.

There was enough pedestrian traffic that Liam could track the four kids easily. In his opinion, it was the essence of good bodyguard work. Let the client live a normal life, without knowing security was even there.

He was mentally patting himself on the back for a good job when the four kids stopped in front of a women's clothing shop at the corner of the Rue des Menuisiers. Ayesha and the other girl went inside, while the boys waited on the street. Then Maks's cell phone rang, and he stepped out into a larger street, one whose name was so long it was printed on the street sign in small letters. Stupid, Liam thought. The kid was going to get himself run over by one of the taxis, trucks, or bicyclists clogging the souk.

A dusty white van came barreling down the larger street as if ready to run Maks down where he stood. Liam leaped into action, darting around a taxi and a couple arguing in Arabic. He dashed toward Maks as he realized the side door of the van was opening. The driver wasn't going to hit Maks; he was getting into position so someone in the van could grab the boy.

"Maks!" he shouted, but the boy was so intent on his phone he had shut everything else out.

A light-skinned Arab man leaned out of the van as it closed in on Maks. Liam sprinted ahead, just in time to knock the boy away from the man's outstretched hands.

Maks exclaimed something in his native language as he went tumbling toward the street. Liam grabbed him before he fell. The van accelerated away, the side door slamming shut. It swerved around a stopped taxi, and horns blared.

Ricardo and the two girls rushed up. "Maks! Are you okay?" Ayesha took his hand. "What happened?"

"Maks was almost kidnapped," Liam said. Turning to the boy, he said, "This is why your father wanted you to have security. Do you understand now?" He put his arm around Maks's shoulder and steered him toward the parked SUV, the other three kids clustering behind them.

Incident in a Lovely City

Aidan was working his way through his essays when his cell rang. "We've got a situation," Liam said. "Meet me in front of the monastery in ten."

"Can it wait? I've still got papers to grade."

"No, it can't wait," Liam said, closing the connection.

Aidan frowned. No matter how many times they went over it, Liam didn't seem to understand that Aidan had a job to do—to make sure that these kids could read and write and speak better English in six weeks. And of course he was typically closemouthed; Aidan had no idea if Liam had spotted another mysterious prowler, had another tiff with Maks, or whether something dangerous had happened.

One look at Liam's face, though, as the SUV pulled into the forecourt, and Aidan knew it was serious. "What's up?" he asked as the kids spilled out into the driveway.

"Someone try to kidnap Maks!" Ayesha said. "In the souk. But Liam stop him."

"Let's sit down and talk this out," Liam said, nodding toward a round stone table in the courtyard.

He and Aidan sat on one stone bench, the four kids on the other.

"I'm sorry; I don't know your name yet," Aidan said to the second girl, who wore a retro sixties dress that screamed Betsy Johnson.

She looked down at the table. "I am Carla," she said. "I am living in Germany, but my family come from Ankara, in Turkey."

A regular little United Nations, Aidan thought. Maks from Turkmenistan, Ricardo from Italy, and Ayesha from Pakistan. They were joined by the greatest common denominator of all—money.

Carla had dark hair in ringlets, artfully applied makeup, and enough gold on her fingers and wrists to ransom a dozen hostages. Ricardo's Gucci logo T-shirt had the brand's signature red and green stripe down the side, while Ayesha wore a pink Miu Miu ultramini and carried a magenta clutch from Loewe—the Spanish leather company.

"Can someone tell me what happened?" Aidan asked.

"I followed Maks and his friends into Bizerte," Liam said. "Ayesha and Carla went into a store, and Maks and Ricardo stayed outside. Then Maks's phone rang." He turned to the boy. "Who called you?"

"No one there," Maks said. "Is not number I know, and no one speak."

"Can I see your phone?" Aidan asked, and Maks gave it to him. Aidan flipped it open and turned to the call log. "This the call?"

Maks nodded.

"It's area code 216," Aidan said. "That's Tunisia. Do you know anyone in this country?"

"No one but school here. I step out to road for better reception, but still nothing."

"Just what they wanted you to do," Liam said. "A white van approached, and I saw hands reaching out the side door. I managed to knock Maks out of the way, and the van kept going."

"Liam was hero," Carla said. Aidan could see the worship in her eyes.

"The call was probably from a prepaid cell phone, if the person who called you was in the van," Aidan said. "I'll try and track the number anyway." He pulled out his red marking pen and copied the number onto a blank piece of paper.

"None of you should say anything about this," Liam said. "Do you understand? We don't want to get anyone worried or upset. Aidan and I will step up our game and make sure Maks is safe."

Ayesha looked at Aidan. "You are security also? Not teacher?"

"I'm both," Aidan said. "Carla, Ayesha, and Ricardo, why don't you guys go get ready for dinner. Maks can stay here while we call his father."

"No, please," Maks said. "If you are telling my father, he will make me leave."

"Sorry, Maks," Liam said as the other three students stood up. "We're working for your father. It's our responsibility to tell him what's going on."

Liam dialed the number Ullyanov had given him. When the assistant answered, Liam gave him a brief recap of what had happened.

"This is not good," Aidan heard Ullyanov say. "Mr. Bazarov is in meeting. I tell him and call you back."

Maks slumped, his elbows resting on the stone table.

"Do you know any reason why someone would want to kidnap you or hurt you?" Aidan asked gently.

"Ullyanov said something about some demonstrations for one of your teachers?" Liam asked.

"Mr. Atayev," Maks said. "He is arrested, and we protest."

"What does that mean, protest?" Liam asked. "What did you do?"

Maks opened his mouth, but nothing came out. Aidan could see he was trying to think of the words. "What language do you speak besides English?" he asked the boy.

"My language. And Arabic. My nurse, she speak with me always."

"Can you say it better in Arabic?" Aidan asked. "We won't tell Madame Abboud."

Maks nodded gratefully and launched into his story in Arabic. "I studied at the International School in Ashgabat. My favorite teacher was Mr. Atayev, who taught history and social science. He was very passionate about Turkmen history, the Turkmen people. How we had been held back by the Russians for many years."

After studying Arabic for a year by then, Aidan understood most of what the boy said.

"What happened?" Liam asked.

"He was arrested in March," Maks said. "For agitating against the state. But he was not a bad man at all. He just wanted rights for all the people of our country. I organized a group of students at my school. We sent e-mails, we posted to Facebook, we made posters and protested by the presidential palace."

He looked at them both. "Have you been to my country?"

Aidan and Liam shook their heads.

"Ashgabat means 'lovely city' in my language. The presidential palace is beautiful, with marble columns and pools of water and a big gold dome."

"Did the government let you protest?" Liam asked.

"There were police all around us, but they let us walk and wave our posters. Then we went home." He frowned. "But the government was not happy. A boy who was on a scholarship at the school had his money taken away, and he had to leave. A girl from Belarus whose father worked at the embassy lost his job, and they went home." He shook his head. "This was very foolish of us. It hurt many people."

"What about you and your family?" Aidan asked in English. "Did anything happen to you?"

Maks followed his lead and returned to English. "Police come to my house to ask questions. But my father very rich and powerful. He make big deal, tell me no more protest or no more school."

"That's all?" Liam asked.

"Yes. But he do say I must leave for college in US early." He looked from Aidan to Liam. "You think this was my country who wish to take me?"

"We don't know," Liam said as his cell phone rang. "This is Ullyanov."

He put the phone on speaker so that Maks and Aidan could hear. "I spoke with Mr. Bazarov," Ullyanov said. "He is very upset. But it will take time to make arrangements for Maks to go elsewhere. He must stay in Tunisia for now. You will protect him?"

"Of course," Liam said.

"I will be careful," Maks said to the phone. "Will you tell my father please I love him and I am sorry for trouble?"

"Your father loves you very much, Maksat," Ullyanov said. "Please be careful with yourself for his sake."

Liam promised to check back with Ullyanov the next day, and ended the call. They sent Maks to get ready for dinner, and climbed the stone stairs together. As Liam stepped into their room, he flexed his back and said, "Hell of a day. Until I saw that van coming, I didn't believe there was a real threat to the kid. But now I do."

"Who do you think it was?"

"I have no idea. And I don't like that."

Aidan stacked his essays on the top of the bureau. "I think it's far-fetched to assume that somebody from Turkmenistan has followed him here to punish him for some kind of protest, don't you?"

"I don't know what to think." Liam looked out the window at the ocean. "I'm sure there's a lot that Bazarov isn't telling us. Can you look for more information online? I'm going to make a couple of phone calls, see if I can dig anything up."

"And we should get Maks to check in with his friends back home. See if any of them have been threatened."

Aidan opened his laptop and started searching while Liam stood by the window and called a friend in the Tunisian police. Aidan found some information on protests in Ashgabat, but most of the articles were in the Turkmen language or in the Cyrillic alphabet. He knew he could dig deeper, but it was time for dinner.

"Faisal's going to see what he can find," Liam said as they walked downstairs. Liam had worked with Faisal Qasim during his time as a SEAL, and it was Faisal who had provided the contact that brought Liam back to Tunisia to set up as a bodyguard.

Maks was sitting with his friends when Liam and Aidan walked into the dining hall. While Liam went over to the buffet line, Aidan slid into the seat next to the teenager.

"About this afternoon," he said.

The incident had frightened the boy. "I am promise, I will be good," Maks said.

"Yes, I believe you. But we want to know more about what's going on. Can you either call or e-mail your friends back home and see if any of them have been threatened too? The ones who protested with you?"

"Yes," Maks said. "I will do that."

"Good. Things will be okay, Maks. You'll see." He patted the boy on the shoulder and went up to join Liam in the food line. They both sat with Maks and his friends, Carla scooting over to make extra room for Liam.

Despite the request to keep the story of Maks' abduction a secret, the kids couldn't stop chattering about the incident at the souk, and Aidan was sure that every student would know about it by the end of the evening. But that was good in a way, because it meant there would be fifty more pairs of eyes and ears looking out for Maks, or at least looking for their own opportunity to take part in his story.

There was another movie showing in the chapel, but Aidan and Liam passed and went up to their room in silence. Aidan felt exhausted and remembered this was the side effect of teaching. How many times had he come back to the apartment he shared in Philadelphia with Blake, emotionally and physically drained?

Sometimes it was because English was a damnably tough language, and it was a struggle to get students to master its intricacies of pronunciation and grammar. Sometimes it was because his students were immigrants who brought their personal problems into the classroom—living far from family, visa problems, lack of money, or poor health.

Did he want to go back to all that? It was tough, yet also rewarding. He had helped students fill out job applications, pass citizenship exams, wire money back to sick relatives. In general, his students had been so grateful for any assistance that he felt almost Scrooge-like when he had to refuse. He couldn't offer shelter to a student who became homeless because he lived with Blake, who owned the apartment and didn't like having company. Sometimes he had to fail even a hard-working student who just didn't have the skills to progress.

But he had new responsibilities now, to Liam and to their clients. Could he go back to teaching and give it less than his full effort? Could he balance both? He didn't know.

Liam fell into sleep almost as soon as they had exchanged their "love yous" and turned off the lights, but Aidan remained awake, considering everything that had happened. He dozed off sometime in the middle of the night, but his dreams continued, and he woke feeling tired and achy. It was a struggle to get up and go downstairs for breakfast.

The food and the coffee revived him, and he was ready to be sociable again when Maks came up to them. "I am check with my friends." He pulled out his cell phone and punched some buttons. Liam and Aidan looked over his shoulder as Maks opened the Facebook application.

Though the words on Maks's page were all in Latin characters, Aidan couldn't make sense of any of them. "I tell what happen," Maks said, pointing at one block of text. "And friends answer."

Maks walked both of them through each of his friends' responses as they ate. None of them had been threatened or been in any danger. Aidan looked at Liam but knew they couldn't speak in front of the boy or any of his classmates.

Aidan went to teach his advanced reading class, where they were working through *Twilight* by Stephenie Meyer. It wasn't his favorite form of literature, but in his experience, kids read better when it was something they liked. He had even arranged to have a DVD of the movie sent over from the States; it would be a nice reward for them, and additional practice for their speaking and listening.

When he met up with Liam at his break between classes, there wasn't much to say. They had no leads and no idea where to look for information. "Can you do some more research online on Bazarov?" Liam asked as they walked through the forecourt.

"I have a couple of papers to look over before the afternoon class, and then I'll get a new set of practice exercises from the kids," Aidan said. "It's a never-ending cycle. The only way for them to learn to write better is to write more—and that means I have papers to grade every day."

"I need to spend some more time going through this property," Liam said. "I want to make sure we seal up any vulnerability. Maks has to be safe while he's here, even if he can't be completely safe outside."

Aidan couldn't help feeling Liam's energy, a high level of alert, as if he radiated something that made the air around him buzz. "It'll be okay," Aidan said, putting his hand on Liam's shoulder. "We'll figure this out."

Aidan taught his afternoon class, then found a quiet place in the chapel where he could grade his papers. His skin was already turning a darker shade of tan after the time he'd spent out at the beach, and he wanted to make sure he didn't burn. He couldn't imagine how Jennifer and Monica could manage—they'd been out there every afternoon since arriving at the monastery, both of them looking increasingly pink-faced despite all the sunscreen they lathered on.

He met up with Liam outside the dining hall just before dinner. Liam still radiated that energy, but it was more subdued. "I think I understand all the weak points of this place, and I'm working on getting them all fixed. How was your day?"

"Today's papers were better than the first set. It usually takes kids a couple of days to warm up when it comes to writing."

They sat with a different group of teens, and after they left, Aidan and Liam were lingering over dessert at one of the long tables when Ismail came up to them. "May I speak with you, please?" he asked.

"Sure," Aidan said. "What's up?"

Ismail sat down. "I am worried that some of our faculty are not presenting the best appearance for the Institute. Have you seen Jennifer and Monica? Every afternoon they are out at the beach in very small bikini bathing suits. It is not proper."

"You should take that up with Madame Abboud," Aidan said. "It's her place to say anything, not mine or Liam's."

"But you support me?"

Aidan looked at Liam, who remained impassive. "I think it's their business," Aidan said. "I'll bet the kids wear bathing suits just as skimpy."

"But that is the point. How are we to retain our authority if the students think we are just like them? If they see their teacher's very large breasts out at the beach?"

That would be Monica, Aidan thought. "Like I said, you should talk to Madame Abboud if it bothers you."

"I will. But I have another complaint as well."

Aidan repressed a sigh. "Yes?"

"I have noticed that Colin drinks alcohol. In his room."

"What were you doing in Colin's room?" Liam asked.

Ismail's coffee-colored skin appeared to darken with a blush. "I was not in his room. But I have observed him several times carrying bottles of wine between his room and the kitchen."

"You've been spying on him?" Liam asked. "Do you think his private behavior concerns you?"

Ismail stood up. "I can see you are not as responsible as I had hoped. I will have to make my concerns known to the proper authorities."

"Let's remember to keep our bedroom door closed," Liam whispered as the Tunisian walked away. "Or else Ismail will be reporting us to the proper authorities too."

"Or we could tie him to the bed, pull down his pants, and remove the broomstick he's got stuck up his ass," Aidan said.

"Or not," Liam said, smiling.

Where There's Smoke

That night Aidan sat up in bed with the institute's schedule. "There's a bus trip to the archaeological park in Carthage on Saturday," he said. "What are we going to do about that?"

"What's there?"

Aidan put the schedule down. "I know the historical stuff about Carthage but not the attractions. Do I look like a guidebook to you?"

"No, you look like you have a laptop next to you. Make with the searching."

Aidan grumbled, but he reached for the computer. One of the few upgrades the monks had done when they converted the monastery into a retreat and conference center had been to install wireless Internet access, and Aidan was able to find some background on the archaeological park.

"Looks like there's a Roman amphitheater, the ruins of some baths, mosaics, graves, yada yada yada."

"What do you think? Should we let Maks go?"

"It's going to be hard to tell Maks that he can't go with the rest of the students. We can't just lock him in his room."

"Maybe his father will pull him out by then."

A whooping noise rose in volume from the hallway. "What the hell?" Aidan said.

"It's the fire alarm," Liam said, jumping up. "I can smell the smoke." He grabbed his vest and his shorts. "I'm going for Maks. You work with the rest of the kids. Remember to take a radio with you." He grabbed one of the two-way radios they had brought with them from Tunis and darted out the door of their room. Aidan heard him banging on doors as he ran down the hall. "Fire alarm! Fire alarm! Everybody up!"

Aidan pulled on his shorts and a T-shirt. At the last minute, he realized he would need a list of the kids, to check them off and make sure all were safe. He rooted in his file folder, and when he couldn't find the roster quickly, he grabbed the whole folder. As he was rushing out the door, he remembered the radio, ran back in the room and grabbed it.

Ismail opened the door to the room he shared with Rashid and looked out as Aidan passed. "What is the trouble?"

"It's a fire. We have to get everyone outside, now!"

Monica and Jennifer stumbled out of their room in nightgowns. "Go, go!" Aidan shouted. He saw Liam banging on Maks's door down the hall.

His brain was filled with conflicting thoughts as he followed Liam. What if this was a direct attempt on Maks? Liam might need his help. Maks's father was paying them, but Aidan felt responsible for each and every kid. He was frightened too; in college, there had been a fire in his dorm, and he remembered the panic, the chaos, the fire trucks with their flashing lights.

"Monica, you and Colin go to the stairs," he said. "Make sure everybody stays calm. Jennifer, Rashid, and Ismail, help me make sure we get every kid out."

They had all been in the classroom long enough to know how to keep order among kids. Jennifer took the girls' rooms, Ismail and Rashid the boys'. Aidan stood in the hallway, moving the kids down the hall.

The fear was palpable in the narrow hallway as the kids chattered and stumbled.

Aidan worried as he shepherded them along. Where was Liam? Had he found Maks? Liam had mentioned there was a back stairway used by the monks, but Aidan didn't know where it was or how to find it.

Ismail approached behind a group of students. "Every room on this side of the hall is empty," he said, motioning to his right. "Jennifer is helping one of the girls who took some sleeping pills, and Rashid is getting the last couple of boys out."

"I'm going downstairs to start checking kids off on the roster." Aidan hurried past a couple of laggards on the staircase, taking the steps two at a time and going so fast he was worried he wouldn't stop when he got to the ground floor.

Kids were filing out into the forecourt, bright as day with the high-intensity lights Liam had installed. The smell of smoke was stronger, and Aidan looked around for Liam but didn't see him. In the distance he heard an approaching siren.

Monica and Colin were already outside, organizing the kids into lines. "We've got to get out of the way of the fire truck," Aidan said. "Get them moving out the driveway."

He went down the lines as they moved toward the street, checking names off. Maks's girlfriend, Ayesha, was holding her friend Carla's hand. "Where is Maks?" Ayesha asked. "I do not see him."

"He's with Liam," Aidan said, more confidently than he felt. "He'll be all right."

By the time the fire engine pulled into the driveway, every kid, every monk, and every staff member was accounted for. All except Liam and Maks.

Aidan pulled the radio from his pocket. "Liam, Liam, come in."

All he heard was static. Where was Liam? Had someone tried to kidnap Maks in the chaos? The fire engine turned into the driveway, sirens blaring and lights flashing, and Aidan had to put the radio away. He spotted Father Antoine talking to the firefighters and walked over toward him.

Remembering that the monk's best languages were Arabic and French, Aidan launched into French. "What happened?" he shouted, after the firemen ran into the monastery.

"A fire in the back courtyard," the monk shouted back over the sound of the siren. "Maybe a student was smoking there."

Suddenly the siren shut off, leaving an echoing silence. A moment later, Aidan heard a woman's voice begin singing, "This land is your land, this land is my land."

It was so disorienting he had to stop, his mouth open. Then more voices joined the first, and he realized the teachers were encouraging the kids to sing. He'd often done that himself in ESL classes, picking simple American folk songs.

The kids weren't standing around a campfire, and there were no marshmallows to roast, but singing was a pretty good idea. He went over to where Monica was leading the singing and joined in. They went through "She'll Be Coming Round the Mountain," "Yankee Doodle," "Greensleeves," and "Tom Dooley" before the firefighters announced the fire had been contained.

Aidan saw the lead fireman talking with Father Antoine, and after the truck pulled away and the kids began climbing back to their rooms, Aidan went over to the old monk. "*Un cocktail Molotov,*" the monk said. Continuing in French, he said, "Who would do such a thing to a holy place, a building filled with children?"

"I don't know, Father," Aidan said, shaking his head, but he thought he had a good idea. When the monk went back inside, he tried the radio again. "Liam, Liam, come in, Liam."

At first there was static again, but then faintly he heard Liam say, "Come in, Aidan."

"Where are you?" Aidan held the radio up to his ear.

"On our way back. Maks is with me. Meet us behind the back gate."

Aidan hurried through the monastery courtyard and cut through the darkened chapel. He got there first, then paced up and down the packed sand, straining to hear any sound over the relentless surf.

A tiny beam of light approached from the direction of Bizerte, and he walked toward it. When Liam and Maks finally came into view, he wanted to run toward Liam and hug him but held back because he didn't want to appear inappropriate or weak in front of the client.

"What was it?" Liam asked.

"We can talk about it upstairs."

"Maks knows there's something going on." Liam put his arm around Maks's shoulder. "He's okay. Right?"

The teenager nodded.

"Father Antoine told me it was a Molotov cocktail," Aidan said.

"A simple way to start a fire," Liam said to Maks. "You put some gasoline in a bottle and stick a piece of cloth in the neck of the bottle to serve as a wick. You set the wick on fire, then throw the bottle."

"Over the back wall," Aidan said. "But how did you get out? I didn't see you go out the front, and the fire was blocking the back gate."

"I found a side door the other day," Liam said. "I made sure it would be good for us to use in emergencies."

"Would have been nice if you'd told me." They all turned to walk back to the monastery.

"Sorry. I was going to take you on a tour this weekend."

"Well, you're both safe," Aidan said. "That's what's important."

They walked Maks in the back gate and locked it behind them, and then escorted him to his room, where Ricardo was waiting up for his return. They began chattering as Liam closed the door.

"This is getting serious," Aidan said. "I think we need to accelerate Bazarov's timetable for getting Maks out of here. Maybe he can go home to Turkmenistan."

"Home isn't necessarily any safer than here."

"But at least at home he's not putting fifty other kids in danger. Not to mention a bunch of monks and teachers."

"I know. I'm worried too."

Back in the bedroom, Aidan felt his adrenaline drain and all he wanted to do was fall into bed. "We'll have to call Bazarov in the morning," Liam said. "He's the client, so he's going to have to call the shots."

"Don't say shots," Aidan said. "So far we've been lucky and there haven't been any guns involved."

"Let's hope our luck holds," Liam said.

In the Pipeline

Liam woke the next morning to a persistent ocean breeze that dissipated much of the smell of smoke and wet wood. The tension, however, still remained. All through breakfast, the students buzzed about the fire, and many of the faculty had to reprimand students to speak English rather than their native languages.

After breakfast, Liam pulled Maks out of his first period class and took him into the chapel, where he called Ullyanov and explained what had happened the night before, about the Molotov cocktail and the subsequent fire.

"You believe this was a threat against Maks?" Ullyanov said.

"It's hard to believe otherwise. First the kidnap attempt in the souk, then this."

"This is very bad," Ullyanov said. "Mr. Bazarov is in Moscow right now, concluding a very important deal. It is necessary that Maks remain safe until that is finished."

"And then?" Liam asked. "Will Mr. Bazarov want Maks to return home?"

"After this deal is signed, there should be no more problems."

"What do you mean?"

"I am sorry. I have said too much already. I must go and speak with Mr. Bazarov."

Ullyanov ended the call.

"You know what that is about?" Liam asked Maks.

He shrugged. "My father, he is always making business."

Liam sent Maks back to class and went upstairs. He did a quick workout in the room, then took a shower. After he was dressed, he collected the laptop and drove down the Cairo-Dakar toward Bizerte until he found the café the Wi-Fi locator on his cell phone had told him offered free access.

He went inside, ordered a cappuccino, and started surfing, reading the *International Herald Tribune* and *Al Horria*, the Arabic-language paper from Tunis. Then he got to work.

He usually left the research to Aidan, but with his partner tied up teaching, he was going to have to take over some of that. He did some quick searching on Bazarov, on his business names, and on Turkmenistan in general. There was nothing that he and Liam didn't already know about.

But there was some kind of deal in the works—a deal that was due to be signed on Monday. It had to be something important if someone was threatening Bazarov's son. But what could it be?

He finished his cappuccino and ordered another, reading through page after page of increasingly random and useless information on Bazarov, his businesses, and Turkmen politics. In a report on natural gas extraction in the Turkmen desert, he read about a plan to build a pipeline to move the gas under the Caspian Sea to Chechnya. As of the date of the report, it had stalled.

But with that information in hand, he was able to focus his search better, and in a Cairo newspaper, he found a report on negotiations for the pipeline. The major oil and gas companies in Turkmenistan were ranging behind two different plans: one from the Soviets and one from the Chinese.

Bells started ringing in Liam's brain. That was the kind of decision companies would fight over—and it wouldn't take much to make that kind of fight personal. He followed links and researched the two competing companies. There was little information on the Chinese one; it was owned, in large part, by the government, and the Chinese kept a tight rein on information that went out on the Internet. Liam couldn't read Chinese, either, and the free translation tools online didn't make much sense out of what he did find.

He had more luck with the Russian company, Stroika Popov, which had built several pipeline projects through parts of the former Soviet Union. It was owned by a man named Ruslan Popov, who had a reputation for flaunting his wealth. *Forbes* estimated his net worth at somewhere over six billion dollars. He owned a home in the ritzy Moscow neighborhood of Christie Prudy, near the Kremlin, and one online site had called him a "Blingshevik," combining Bolshevik and bling.

Liam found a few whispers that Popov's wealth was based in criminal activity, but there was no real proof, and the information could have been mere jealousy.

Were the threats against Maks connected to these contract negotiations? Were the Russians or the Chinese involved? Or maybe some unknown third party? There had been two attempts to kidnap Maks in two days. Whoever was after the boy was upping the ante.

Liam stayed at the café through lunch, and when he returned to the monastery, classes were letting out. He checked on Maks, who said he would spend the afternoon in his room playing a video game with Ricardo. He found Aidan in their room.

"Madame Abboud is here, and she wants to meet with everyone in the chapel at four," Aidan said. It was two thirty then.

"Shit. I need you to look over this information I found. We'll have to make it quick."

He set up the laptop and brought up the sites he had bookmarked. "Read this stuff," he said to Aidan. "I'm going to take a quick look around."

He checked the back and side gates and walked around the perimeter wall. By the time he returned, Aidan had read most of the material. He looked up when Liam walked in and said, "You think this is the contract negotiation Ullyanov mentioned?"

"Makes sense, doesn't it?"

"But which side is after Maks?"

"Don't know. I'm thinking we should call Ullyanov again and confront him."

They went back and forth over the question. It was one thing to ask for information that was important to a case, but another to interfere with a client's business. And the threat to Maks could be unrelated to the contract, which would only make Bazarov angry. By four, they had come to no decision.

The stone stairway was cool; the monks had been smart about its construction, with only narrow windows that let light in but kept the heat out. Leaving the main building, however, was another story; the sun was bright and hot and shimmered over the paving stones in the courtyard.

Liam and Aidan hurried through the heat to the chapel, back into the sanctuary of cool stone. The west-facing stained-glass window of St. Augustine in the garden where he underwent his conversion sent multicolored shards of light onto the stone floor.

Madame Abboud had brought some wine with her from Tunis, and when Aidan and Liam walked in, the rest of the faculty were already there, standing in front of the altar drinking and making conversation.

"Ah, we are all safe now," Madame Abboud said. "Our bodyguards are here!"

She hurried up and kissed Aidan on each cheek. Liam had to bend at the waist so she could do the same for him. "I understand we had some drama?"

"Nothing we couldn't handle." Liam wasn't going to justify his actions to her. "I'll get us some wine," he said to Aidan, leaving him to explain what had happened to Madame Abboud.

Liam wasn't comfortable with small talk. It was a skill they didn't teach in SEAL training, and that meant, to him at least, it wasn't worthwhile. So he stood around awkwardly as the faculty chattered about students and teaching strategies.

He finished his wine and put the plastic glass down on the table, then stood at parade rest. Monica and Jennifer broke away from laughing with Colin to come up to Liam.

"Explain to us exactly why we have a bodyguard here," Jennifer demanded. Liam could tell she'd had a couple of drinks already. "What's so dangerous?"

"I'm here to protect one of the students," Liam said. "His father is wealthy and concerned for his safety."

"He's talking about Maks Bazarov," Monica said. "He comes from one of those Stans, you know. Babookistan or Malikistan or somewhere. Everybody who has any money in those places is crooked."

Liam was surprised that a woman with a master's degree, traveling around Europe and Africa, had such a limited grasp of geography and such a narrow attitude about foreign countries and their people, but he didn't say anything.

Monica was wearing a low-cut blouse that showed off her large breasts, which glowed with sunburn. He wondered if she sunbathed topless and what Madame Abboud would think about that. Perhaps that was why Ismail had complained the night before.

"So what's up with you and Aidan?" Monica asked. "He's gay, you know."

"I know."

"Usually big butch guys like you don't like gay guys," Monica said. "Aren't you some kind of soldier?"

Liam had been taught since he was a child never to strike a woman—and he never would, unless he had to in a combat situation. But Monica was the kind of annoying pest who needed to be slapped down. The only way he could do it, though, was with words.

"I was a Navy SEAL," Liam said. "I left the service because I violated Don't Ask, Don't Tell." He smiled at her. "I started my own bodyguard business in Tunis. Then I fell in love with Aidan and he came to work with me."

Monica's mouth gaped open. "I told you," Jennifer said, elbowing her. "You never listen to me."

Fortunately Madame Abboud clapped her hands and said, "It is time we go in to dinner. But don't worry, we will take the extra wine with us."

They sat at the head table once more, probably so that the students wouldn't see the faculty getting tipsy. Liam was grateful that Jennifer and Monica were at the far end of the table, but the price he paid was sitting with Madame Abboud.

"I am disturbed by these dangers," she said to Aidan and Liam as they ate their pasta, served once again by the kitchen staff. "Perhaps it would be better if Maks were to leave."

"His father says things will clear up after a contract is signed on Monday," Liam said.

"Ah, but I have seen the way these business contracts are signed, or not signed," Madame Abboud said. "They say Monday, but it does not happen."

"What if we took Maks to a hotel somewhere for the weekend?" Aidan asked. "And then we could bring him back on Monday when his father says everything is fine. Or we could just wait with him there."

"But what about your teaching?" Madame Abboud said.

"I'll come back on Monday to teach," Aidan said.

"It would be inconvenient." She picked at her dish. "There is the field trip tomorrow, and I would suffer not to have you both there."

Liam began thinking of ways to make Madame Abboud suffer as she continued to chatter on. "No, no, I think it best that Maks stay with the group," she said finally. "This is the agreement I have with his father."

Liam resisted drinking any more wine with dinner, especially once he realized Aidan was continuing to drink. There was another movie after dinner, *Saving Private Ryan*, and Aidan and Liam sat out in the courtyard with the students to watch. Within a couple of minutes, though, Aidan had dozed off. Liam was irritated; he wanted to be able to get up and walk around the property, keeping an eye out for any new threats, but he couldn't leave the kids alone with Aidan asleep.

Aidan seemed to be changing more with every day he spent as a teacher. He'd never have gotten drunk on a bodyguard assignment. And he'd never stood up to Liam before, at least not in the way he had about maintaining his focus on teaching.

Fuck it. He'd just gotten comfortable living with and loving one Aidan. Was there going to be a new guy inside Aidan's body he'd have to learn to deal with? Or was the real Aidan just now coming out? What if the man Liam had fallen in love with had just been a mask, Aidan making the best of a new situation by trying to be what Liam wanted?

What if he didn't know the true Aidan at all?

The movie began with a long sequence of the brutal assault on Omaha Beach, and every time a gun blasted or a bomb exploded, Liam shifted uncomfortably. What a stupid choice for a movie, he thought. But of course no one had known in advance that there would be any threats. It was just bad luck.

He had never been superstitious before he joined the SEALs. But years of operations had shown him that sometimes, no matter how carefully you planned, things went wrong. If your stars were out of alignment or your luck turned bad, a whole operation could go into the toilet. And he had a bad feeling about this job.

Aidan roused at the end of the movie, and Liam sent him up to the room. "Love you. You hit the hay. I'm going to do a last patrol."

He checked each lock and each door. He walked the beach up and down with a high-intensity flashlight, searching for unusual marks or footprints. He found nothing, though that did not quell his uneasiness.

Roadblock

Saturday morning Aidan packed two bags of gear to take with them on the bus trip to Carthage. In went two-way radios, bottled water, a map, and bags of trail mix.

Liam leaned down and pulled their two pistols from an improvised hiding place under the bed. "I don't think we'll need extra ammunition," he said.

"Are you sure we need guns at all? It's a school field trip, not a military operation."

"We're on high alert. If anything goes down, I want a weapon available."

"You're going to be surrounded by fifty teenagers," Aidan protested. "You won't be able to draw a gun."

"Leave that to me. Just pack the guns."

They carried the bags down to the dining hall, where they ate breakfast at the table that had become their regular one, with Maks, Ricardo, Ayesha, and Carla. "The city we're going to, Carthage, was a very important one in literature," Aidan said. "It's a major location in Virgil's *Aeneid*, as Aeneas arrives in Carthage and becomes a favorite of its queen, Dido."

"Is that not the English word for sex toy?" Ricardo asked. "Dido?"

"That's dildo," Aidan said, trying and failing to suppress a laugh.

The grinding of gears resounded through the dining hall. Liam stood up. "That must be the bus. I'm going to check it out." He hefted both of the bags and strode out.

Liam had been abrupt and irritable ever since the kidnap attempt in the souk, Aidan thought, watching him go. It wasn't just the threat to Maks; there was something more. In the past year, whenever there had been a problem with a client, he and Liam had worked together as a unit. That wasn't happening now.

Was it him, he wondered as he dawdled over his coffee. He felt different now that he had returned to teaching. He didn't love Liam any less, but he did like making his own decisions about what to teach, how to handle problems, and so on. Perhaps he had been deferring to Liam too much about those things when it came to the bodyguard business.

But Liam was the expert there, and so it had seemed natural to go along with what he wanted. And Aidan had long ago accepted the fact that he was a beta male—the kind of guy who liked being subservient to an alpha like Liam. With his ex, Blake, Aidan had been the housewife, bowing to Blake's wishes when it came to restaurants, vacations, even the clothes he himself wore.

Was he recreating those same patterns with Liam? He had started working out like Liam after they met, dressing like Liam. He had changed the kind of food he prepared to suit Liam's appetites and tastes.

Yet in the classroom, he was the boss. It was probably the only place in his life where he was really in charge. Was that what he liked about it? Not the actual process of teaching, the chance to help people? Just having someone he could boss around for a change?

It was too much to think about, so he gave up and followed Liam outside. It was just after eight o'clock as he stepped out into the courtyard to another sunny day, though cooler than they were accustomed to in Tunis. He knew it would get hotter as they drove south and inland, and imagined the students would have limited interest in prowling the museum grounds and the cemetery in the midday heat.

A large tour bus—big enough to accommodate all fifty students and the faculty as well—pulled up outside the front door and ground to a halt. Liam handed one of the bags to Aidan as they walked behind the crowd of kids. "We're going in the SUV, Maks," Liam called to the teen as they came out into the courtyard.

"No, no," Madame Abboud said, appearing behind them. "You must all ride in the bus. It is our liability agreement. I cannot have students in separate vehicles."

Liam started to protest, but Aidan put a hand on his arm. "Pick your battles," he said. "We'll be right there in the bus with him."

"Fine."

Aidan knew it wasn't fine with Liam at all, but his partner was smart enough to recognize it would be more trouble than it was worth to get into a fight with

Madame Abboud in front of the student body. Liam paced the courtyard like a caged animal as the students and faculty filed onto the bus, Aidan checking names on the roster. When they were sure everyone was on board, they climbed on themselves and made their way to seats at the rear of the bus.

Aidan was looking forward to the trip. He had been grading papers each evening until he was cross-eyed, and he wanted to have a simple day, just hanging out with the kids and not worrying about their command of grammar or vocabulary. They were a good bunch, and he doubted they'd make much trouble.

It would be nice to spend the day with Liam too. Maybe they could work out whatever seemed to be going wrong between them. They'd hang out, have a few laughs, maybe even get themselves in the mood for sex later that night. That always seemed to bring them together.

They approached the left turn that would take them to the highway, and a dirty white van drove toward them, pulling up right in front of them. Aidan saw that the bus driver tried to wave the van to one side, but the van's driver did not move.

"Goddamn it," Liam said. "I think that's the same van that tried to grab Maks in the souk."

The bus driver cursed in Arabic and looked behind them. Aidan turned around and saw a khaki-colored pickup truck come to a stop behind them. Four men armed with rifles spilled out of the back.

"Shit. Look behind us," Aidan whispered to Liam.

"It's an ambush. We've got to play it cool, though."

Two more armed men got out of the van and ran up to the bus door. One of them, tall and dark-haired, rapped his handgun against the glass door. Aidan felt his pulse rate accelerate.

"What is going on?" Madame Abboud demanded in Arabic, abandoning her English-only policy. "Do not open that door."

The driver shook his head at the gunman, who stepped back, and aimed his gun at the glass door. With a loud bang the glass shattered, and kids on the bus began to scream.

"What can we do?" Aidan whispered to Liam.

"Damn it, we should have insisted on taking Maks in the SUV. There are too many kids in front of us now. I'd never get a clear shot. You were right about that this morning."

The lead gunman knocked the door open, and Madame Abboud shrieked at him.

"Quiet!" he shouted in Arabic. Aidan could tell his accent was rough, but he didn't know why. Madame Abboud cowered back in her seat, and the kids quieted themselves to whimpers.

Aidan felt sweat breaking out on his forehead and his back. Carefully he pulled his cell phone from his pocket. He didn't know the phone number for the local police, though; that was a detail they had overlooked in their planning.

"Where is Maksat Bazarov?" the gunman demanded again in Arabic.

Aidan could see Liam evaluating his chances for a shot, but it was clear that none would be available.

There were so many men outside that even if he shot the man at the front of the bus, his comrades would surely respond. There would be bloodshed, innocent teenagers hurt and possibly killed.

Aidan looked forward to where Maks sat, and saw him slowly raise his hand. He was sitting halfway back in the bus, in an aisle seat.

"You come with me," the gunman said.

Maks looked around. Aidan could see fear in his eyes, but he felt helpless to do anything to help the kid. From the energy rising off Liam like a fever, he could tell his partner felt the same way.

Maks turned back toward the front of the bus and began walking down the aisle. "No, Maks, don't go," Ayesha said. "They will hurt you."

Maks hesitated, and the gunman barked again. "Now!"

Maks made his way down the narrow aisle. Ricardo reached out to grasp his hand, which Maks slapped in a shaky high five. When he reached the front of the bus, the gunman stepped back outside, waving Maks to follow him. With one look back, Maks got off the bus.

"You have the digital camera?" Liam whispered to Aidan, who dug it out of his pack and handed it over.

Liam hurried up the aisle to the front of the bus as the four men returned to the truck behind them, and the two men from the van led Maks to it and shoved him in the back. The students erupted in excited chatter as Liam took a series of photos of the gunmen and the van.

Colin was in the row ahead of Aidan. He pulled out his cell phone and said, "I'm calling the police."

"Good," Aidan said. He stood up, then began moving down the aisle, carrying both his bag and Liam's. It was awkward maneuvering past the kids, who had all begun to stand up and chatter and cry.

"You must stop them!" Madame Abboud said, pushing against Liam's shoulder as the van whipped around and took off down the road. "Maks is under my care!"

They were only about a quarter mile from the monastery. "We're going back," Liam said to Madame Abboud as Aidan came up the aisle toward him. "You all stay here until the police arrive." He looked at the digital screen of the camera and read off the license plate number of the van, which Aidan copied down and handed to Madame Abboud.

"Give that to the police when they come. We'll find Maks and bring him back."

Grabbing one of the bags from Aidan, Liam took off toward the monastery. Aidan followed him. It was a quick jog back to their SUV, in the monastery's forecourt, but Aidan wasn't accustomed to that kind of run in the hot sun, especially not while carrying a bag loaded with gear.

Liam sped ahead, and Aidan stumbled. Why couldn't he have stayed in the bus? Why couldn't he just be a teacher like the others? And why didn't Liam wait for him to catch up? Honestly the man was so self-centered sometimes.

"Wait there!" Liam called. He was almost at the monastery driveway by then. "I'll pick you up!"

Aidan stopped by the side of the road and dropped the bag. He lowered his head and gasped for breath. This was just the kind of crazy thing that had happened when he first met Liam. He had been caught up in Liam's world, and it had seemed fun and sexy and adventurous. Now, though, he wasn't so sure. The bus was air-conditioned, and all he'd have to do was keep rein on a bunch of teenagers.

But he had made a commitment to Maks's father, just as Liam had, and he was worried about the boy's safety. He would have to see this through.

He was still panting when Liam pulled the SUV out of the driveway and turned toward where he stood. He hoisted the bag up and tossed it in the back. "You think we can catch them?" he said as he jumped into the front seat next to Liam.

"It's worth a try."

Liam accelerated the SUV down the street, scattering pebbles, and swung onto the road where the bus had turned. He pulled up next to it. "Did you see which way they went?" he shouted in Arabic, through the shattered glass door.

"Toward Bizerte," the driver said.

Madame Abboud started to say something about responsibility, but Liam waved his hand and accelerated forward. He didn't even pause at the highway intersection, just swung the SUV east and pressed down on the gas. They darted around trucks and rental cars as Liam said, "Call Ullyanov and let him know what happened."

Aidan opened his phone. He had added Ullyanov's number as soon as they got the contract, and he pressed the dial button. The phone rang four times, then connected to voice mail. The message began in a language that was completely foreign to Aidan, but fortunately Ullyanov repeated it in English and Arabic. "Maks has been taken," Aidan said. "Please call me as soon as you get this message."

He ended the call, then dialed another number from his contact list. The man who answered growled, "Do you know what bloody time it is?"

"Sorry to call so early, Richard," Aidan said. He looked at his watch. It was the same time in London as it was in Tunisia, about eight thirty in the morning. "I need a trace on a license plate, ASAP."

Richard was a hacker Liam had known for a few years, skilled at breaking through any firewall. They only used his services in emergencies because what he did was highly illegal—and also very expensive.

Richard yawned. "Read away, mate."

Aidan read off the plate number for the van and listened as Richard's fingers tapped his keyboard. Liam slowed as they passed a turnoff, looking both ways for signs of the van. When he saw nothing, he accelerated again.

"The plate is licensed to an outfit based at the Tunis airport," Richard said. "You'd better hope they've got a decent computer system. Can't do anything for you if they keep paper records."

Liam swerved around a slow-moving truck, still scanning both sides of the road. In a minute, Richard was back on the line. "The plate belongs to a 2010 Toyota Camry. You need renter information?"

"Shit. Not a white van?"

"Sorry, mate. Not the car you were looking for?"

"Not even close." He looked over at Liam. "Any ideas?"

"He must have swapped the plates," Liam said. "It's what I'd do."

Aidan stared out the front window of the SUV as they approached Bizerte and a family of German tourists blindly stepped into the road. Liam slammed on the brakes and honked the horn, and the family scampered across the pavement.

"They let anybody into this damn country," Liam said.

That ignited the spark of an idea. Aidan asked, "Richard, can you get into Tunisian customs and immigration records?"

"I'm insulted you even have to ask."

"Can you do a search for anyone arriving on a passport from Turkmenistan since Sunday? Look for anything that might raise a flag?"

"That'll take a few minutes. I'll call you back."

Aidan disconnected the call as they entered the urban area of Bizerte. He scanned the streets around them. There was no sign of the van.

"I'm going to make a circuit through town," Liam said. "Maybe we'll get lucky." He looked over at Aidan. "What made you ask about immigration records?"

"Bazarov told us that Maks is in danger because of something that happened in Turkmenistan. If that's the case, then our kidnapper is most likely someone on a Turkmen passport."

"That's a pretty big leap. Remember how Ullyanov let it slip that he thought Maks would be safe after Monday. That implies that he thinks it's connected to this contract."

"Either way, it's worth a shot." As they were crossing the bridge over the canal that led into the Vieux Port, Aidan said, "You said that you'd swap the plates on the van, right? So that means this guy is a professional. You need to start thinking like he would."

"Professional kidnapper, you mean. I'm nothing like that."

"Come on, Liam. You've told me stories. We're not talking about morality here; we're talking operations."

Liam didn't say anything at first, just gripped the steering wheel. "If Maks was kidnapped to put pressure on his father to sign a contract, then the kidnapper needs to hide him until Monday."

"I agree. They'd need some kind of hidey-hole. If I were them, I'd rent an apartment rather than go to a hotel. Someplace in a seedy neighborhood where nobody pays attention to who comes and goes."

"Too many places like that in Tunis," Liam said.

Aidan's cell phone rang. "Got you a suspect," Richard said. "Nazar Rakhimov. Turkmenistan passport." He read off the number to Aidan, who copied it down. "Only there's one little problem. Nazar Rakhimov died at age two, twelve years ago. Fucker used a fake passport. What's this world coming to, I ask you?"

"Is there a picture with the passport?" Liam asked.

"That Liam there?" Richard asked. "How you doing, bud?"

"Piss-poor," Liam said.

"Yeah, there's a photo," Richard said. "Ugly bugger. Dark hair, broken nose."

"Scar over the left temple?" Liam asked.

"You're a bloody mind reader, you are," Richard said.

"Just saw him," Liam said. "Can you e-mail us the picture?"

"Done. I've got some nifty image-recognition software. Want me to give it a go?"

"Anything you can do helps," Aidan said.

"May take a while. I'll call you back."

Richard disconnected. They were driving behind a bus with a motorcycle and sidecar painted on the back, an ad for some movie Aidan couldn't decipher, when Liam said, "This is useless. We're never going to find them."

"Then what do we do?"

"You brought the laptop, didn't you? See if there's a place around here we can get Wi-Fi. At least we'll be able to download this bastard's picture."

"I wish Ullyanov would call. We need something to go on." Aidan used the Wi-Fi locator app on his phone and directed Liam to a café near the Gare Routiere, the Bizerte bus station. It was a grimy place, but they ordered bottles of cold soda and pulled up a table by the window.

Poor Maks, Aidan thought as the computer booted up and connected to the Internet. It was a slow connection and that gave him way too much time to think about the teenager and worry about where he was.

Doppelgänger

Liam drummed his fingers on the cheap wooden table as Aidan logged in to his e-mail program and waited while the message from Richard downloaded, with the photo attached.

"We won't get anywhere if you break the table," Aidan said. "Chill out."

"A boy in our care was kidnapped, Aidan. What part of this situation don't you understand?" Liam caught his breath. "I'm sorry. It's not your fault. I screwed up, and it's making me crazy."

He had been put in a reactive position, and he hated that. He also hated that anyone had gotten the slip on him, and the fact that a client he'd been hired to protect had been kidnapped really messed with his head.

"You didn't screw up. You did the best you could with the information you had. Now we'll make things right."

While the photo was downloaded, Aidan went up to the counter and ordered them both cappuccinos. The espresso machine was new and shiny, and there was a constant line of customers. Liam watched as the photo gradually appeared on the screen. He was staring at it when Aidan returned with the coffees.

"That's him," Aidan said, pointing at the scar over the man's left temple. "His hair was shorter, and he had more of a five o'clock shadow. But that's him."

"You always have a good eye when it comes to men," Liam said.

"Too bad I didn't get a closer look at his crotch."

"You'd probably have kicked him there." Liam sipped his cappuccino, the caffeine beginning its run through his system.

"If I could have gotten closer, I would have." The laptop beeped to announce another e-mail had arrived, and he clicked the envelope.

Richard had used his image-recognition software to match the mystery man's face to a file of KGB operatives that had found its way into the public domain after the fall of the Soviet Union. The kidnapper's name was Murat Dvorkin, and he'd been born in Ashgabat in 1961, when Turkmenistan was still a Soviet republic.

They moved closer together to read Dvorkin's dossier. His father was a Russian soldier who had been killed in a military operation when Murat was five years old. His mother, a Muslim woman native to Ashgabat, died a year later, and Murat was placed in an orphanage in the capital, where he lived until he joined the Soviet Army at seventeen.

"You were right," Liam said. "He was a soldier." He scanned the café, conscious of the danger implied by the information on the screen. No one else looked European or American; the other patrons probably worked in the neighborhood or were patrons of the bus terminal across the street. Two young guys with tiny netbooks were surfing the Internet. No one was paying any attention to him or Aidan.

Liam went back to the record. Murat Dvorkin had been stationed in Afghanistan during the Soviet invasion, and when his tour of duty ended, he transferred to the KGB and returned to Ashgabat, where he was detailed to the Soviet embassy. There was a list of operations he was suspected of taking part in. Liam recognized a couple of them, including an attack on alleged Chechen rebels.

"Chechnya," Aidan said, pointing at the screen. "Isn't that across the Caspian Sea from Turkmenistan?"

"Yup. There's a gas pipeline running from there to the west. I think the pipeline Bazarov's involved with is supposed to connect with the one there." Liam sipped his coffee again. A pair of men in overalls came into the café, arguing in Arabic about a problem with bus maintenance. Liam looked at them long enough to establish that they weren't going to break into a fight in the tiny café, and then went back at the computer screen.

The record ended nearly five years before, when Dvorkin had been discharged from the KGB. At the bottom of the message, Richard had copied a single paragraph from a source that had been redacted. Certain words and sentences were blacked out, but they could tell it was a report on Dvorkin's business activities in Ashgabat. He was technically a private investigator, but the report indicated he was more of a fixer—a man who had knowledge of Turkmen business and politics and could make things happen for his clients.

"He has an impressive background," Aidan said. "He reminds me a lot of you."

"Why do you keep trying to make it sound like this jerk is like me?"

"He has a military background like you; he's a private operative like you; and we already know he's damn good at what he does."

Liam glared at Aidan. Dvorkin was some kind of amoral soldier of fortune. That wasn't the way Liam saw himself at all.

Aidan went back to the Internet browser and began searching for information on Murat Dvorkin. Suddenly Liam couldn't stand the confines of the tiny café. He had to get out.

"I'm going outside. Call me back in if you find anything."

The air was heavy with the heat and the smell of bus exhaust. An air conditioner rumbled somewhere nearby, its noise mixing with the sound of traffic and tinny Arabic music coming from a store's open door.

He paced up and down in front of the café. It pissed him off that Aidan kept comparing him to Dvorkin. Sure, he'd done some things as a soldier he wasn't proud of, but he had always been following orders, and as a SEAL he often didn't know the full implications of his actions. What seemed wrong in the immediate context might have been the only logical and moral thing to do when you considered the long run.

Since going out on his own, he had been careful to vet his clients. He wouldn't do anything against the law, and he wouldn't work for anyone he considered shady. It had cost him more than a few lucrative assignments, but he was able to sleep at night.

He looked through the window, and Aidan motioned him back inside. "It's like the guy doesn't exist," Aidan said when Liam sat down next to him. "Nothing. No Google matches, no Web site or Facebook page."

"Try the alias Richard gave you."

Aidan typed in Nazar Rakhimov, and they waited. Over eight thousand results came up. "Sorry, forgot the quotation marks." Aidan added them and clicked the search button again. There were no results.

"He must use multiple aliases." Liam shook his head. "I don't like this at all. Let's call Ullyanov again."

Liam opened his phone and dialed the number but got voice mail again. "We believe Maks has been abducted by a man named Murat Dvorkin. He's an operative out of Ashgabat. But we don't know what he wants Maks for. Let me know immediately if you hear from him."

He slapped the phone shut and started drumming his fingers on the table again.

"Stop that, please," Aidan said. "You're going to give me a headache."

"I need to do something, Aidan. I can't just sit around."

"Put yourself in his shoes, then. You get the assignment to kidnap Maks and hold him until his father signs the contract. What do you do?"

Liam pressed his lips together tightly, afraid of getting angry again. But Aidan was right; if you put morality aside, he was a lot like this Dvorkin, and he should be able to use that to their advantage. He struggled to insert himself into the situation—and then realized what was wrong.

"You're starting too far into the op," he said. "The assignment wouldn't be to kidnap Maks. The assignment would be to put pressure on Bazarov to sign the contract."

"Same thing."

"No, it's not." He spread his hands out on the table. "The first step is to research Bazarov and see where his weakness is. We already know that, but Dvorkin had to learn it—he had to see all those businesses named after Maks and identify him as the target. I'll bet he made some move on Maks in Ashgabat—which is why Bazarov wanted him out of the country."

"Let me write this down," Aidan said. He opened a new document on the computer and started typing.

Liam looked out the window, thinking. "Dvorkin found out about this English course and followed Maks to Tunis, and then to Bizerte. He must have spent a couple of days watching the monastery, and when Maks went into town on Wednesday afternoon, he followed and set up the grab."

"Which you foiled."

"Yes. And he made a key mistake—he showed us that he's not working alone. He had to have help to drive the van, for starters. And he either didn't know that Bazarov hired us, or he didn't realize I was there looking after Maks that day."

Aidan typed. "He does his groundwork," he said. "He got hold of the van and swapped the license plates, and he got the prepaid cell phone. He must have had a place set up for them to take Maks at that point."

"He made his second move with the Molotov cocktail on Thursday night. I'll bet he had the van parked somewhere close to the monastery."

"He must have been getting pretty frustrated by then," Aidan said.

Liam shook his head. "The guy's a professional. He doesn't get frustrated; he just looks ahead to the next couple of moves."

"He must have local contacts," Aidan said. "There were four guys in the truck that pulled up behind the bus, and at least one more guy with him in the van. How does somebody from out of town find that help?"

"Rajif Khan," Liam said.

"I know that name. He's some kind of crook, isn't he?"

"Not so much a crook as a fixer," Liam said. "Kind of like Dvorkin is in Ashgabat. Why didn't I think of him sooner? He'd have a way to get Dvorkin the van, switch the license plates, supply the extra manpower."

"How do we get to Khan?"

"Not so easy. The police have been after him for years, but he's tough to pin down."

"Dvorkin got to him."

"Then we can too." Liam flipped open his phone and called Faisal Qasim, his friend in the Tunisian national police. "Salaam aleikum, my friend," Liam said, switching with ease into Arabic, which had become his second language.

"*Aleikum salaam*," Faisal said. "How are you on this fine Saturday morning?"

"Not as fine as I would like. I need to find Rajif Khan."

Faisal snorted. "Wouldn't we all."

"Yes, but you want to arrest him. I just want to talk to him."

"I've seen the way you talk to people, Liam. What do you need with Khan?"

Liam gave him the short version of the story. "You have reported this to the police in Bizerte?" Faisal asked.

"Of course. But this boy was under my protection when he was taken. I have a moral obligation to retrieve him."

"And you feel Khan will lead you to this missing boy?"

"I don't know. But I don't know anyone else who the kidnapper could get help from on the ground."

"Let me make a few calls."

The Tunisian disconnected, and Liam lay the phone on the table. It rang again almost immediately, and Liam snatched it up without even looking at the display. "Faisal?"

"Now as far as I know, the proper greeting in Arabic is salaam aleikum, not Faisal. Unless they're talking a strange version of Arabic down there in Tunisia these days."

"Sheridan?"

"Who the fuck else? Say, Faisal isn't your boyfriend, is he? Thought you were hooked up with that English teacher who was in the hospital with you."

"Lower your fucking voice, Sheridan," Liam said. Joey Sheridan had been Liam's best friend in the SEALs. "Jesus, you still don't have a volume control, do you? And no, Faisal is not my boyfriend. Don't you remember Faisal Qasim, you dumb redneck?"

"Oh, that Faisal," Joey said. "What are you doing with him?"

"I'm in the middle of a situation here, Sheridan. This a social call?"

"You bet your butt it is. I've got a couple of days leave, and there's a transport leaving for Tunis I can hitch a ride on. I was thinking of crashing at your place."

Liam was thrown for a loop. He'd spoken to Joey a couple of times since leaving the SEALs, and the last time they'd met was on an operation in the desert, the first job he had worked with Aidan on. They'd exchanged e-mails and made vague plans to get together. He appreciated the way that Joey was reaching out—but this wasn't the time.

While Liam stared at the table, unsure how to respond, Aidan reached over and took the phone from him, holding the phone out so Liam could hear. "Hey,

Joey, it's Aidan. The English teacher. We're not in Tunis right now. We're working on a job in Bizerte, on the northern coast."

"Bizerte? Isn't that the place you and I did that op, Billy? You up to anything fun?"

Liam took the phone back. "You're a nut job, you know that? No, it's nothing fun. We were hired to protect a teenage kid, and he got snatched from under our noses."

"Typical Billy McCullough fuckup," Joey said. "Seems like you need me to come down there and pull your ass out of the fire. I can be on the ground in Tunis by two o'clock. Say I make my way up to Bizerte, and I call you and we rendezvous."

"Thanks for the offer, buddy, but we've got it covered."

Aidan took the phone again. "Liam's full of shit, as usual," he said, holding it out of Liam's reach. "We can use your help. And we've got to head down to Tunis ourselves later. Call this number when you land, and we'll swing by the airport."

"Will do. Yee haw." Joey disconnected, and Aidan handed the phone back.

Liam felt anger bubbling up inside him. "You had no fucking right to do that. Sometimes you just go too far, Aidan."

"Whoa. Dial it back a notch. You know we can use Sheridan's help. And it was nice of him to reach out to you like that. When a friend does that, you can't just say no."

"Where's he going to stay? You going to take some time out from hunting down Maks to take him sightseeing?" Liam gritted his teeth. This was why he liked working on his own. Aidan could be a bossy little queen sometimes, and he didn't need this shit right now, while everything was falling apart.

"He's a SEAL, Liam. Like you were. He can sleep on the ground and be happy as a pig in shit, as long as he's getting into trouble. And we've got enough of that to keep him from wanting to go sightseeing."

Liam took a deep breath. "You're right. It's just... I..."

"Let me guess. You don't want him to come to our house and see that we have only one bedroom and one big bed, right? It's one thing to have your buddy know you're gay and another thing to push the evidence in his face?" Aidan's face hardened, and Liam could see he was getting angry. "Or is it me? I'm too gay, aren't I? No matter how many push-ups I can do, how well I can shoot, I'm still queer, and anybody who sees me knows it. And then they know something about you too."

Liam's brain was whirling with too much input. How could Aidan feel that way? Had Liam said or done things to give that impression? He probably had, without even knowing it. What did Joey Sheridan really want? Where was Maks Bazarov? Could Faisal lead them to Rajif Khan, and would Khan know anything?

He closed his eyes and steadied his breathing, practicing techniques that he had learned in the military. When he opened his eyes again, Aidan was still glaring at him.

"I love you, and I'll never be ashamed of you or what anybody thinks about what I do with you," Liam said, though that wasn't completely true. "I'm worried about what Joey will think of me now, not because I'm gay, but because I'm not a SEAL anymore. Joey and I used to make fun of guys who do what you and I do. We called them soldiers of misfortune."

"Sounds like you're talking about Murat Dvorkin, not about you and me," Aidan said. "You and Joey can make fun of Dvorkin all you want, after you track him down and show him who's the boss."

Liam laughed. "You're right, as usual." He looked at his watch. "If we've got to pick up Joey at the airport at two, we'd better get started back to Tunis. I'm sure that's where we'll find Khan, anyway."

"Though I don't want to, I think we're going to have to pass by the monastery first," Aidan said. "Pick up the rest of our gear and tell Madame Abboud what we're doing."

"I'll leave that up to you," Liam said. "If she gives me any grief, I'm likely to try and trade her for Maks with the kidnappers."

When they reached the monastery, though, no one was there beyond Father Antoine and the other monks. "They have taken the students into Carthage," the old monk said.

"She's one cool character," Liam said, shaking his head as they climbed up to their room. "Maks gets kidnapped and she goes on with business as usual."

"Look at it from her perspective," Aidan said. "She's still got forty-nine kids to take care of and keep occupied. If they came back here, with nothing planned, the kids would be nuts before lunch. There would be parents descending in droves, and the whole institute would fall apart."

"If you say so."

They packed everything they had brought with them and loaded it into the back of the SUV. "Tell Madame Abboud I'll call her," Aidan said to Father Antoine in French as he jumped into the passenger seat.

The old monk looked baffled by all that had happened, but he simply nodded his head and waved good-bye to them. Liam envied the monks their air of quiet detachment from the larger world. It was a skill he needed to cultivate.

After this operation was complete, though.

Hanging with Joey

Liam tried to focus on the highway ahead of him, but there were too many other things competing for his attention. Where was Maks? Why wasn't Ullyanov answering his calls? Had the kidnappers already made contact with Bazarov? And would Aidan ever shut up about getting hold of Madame Abboud and asking her to find someone to cover his classes?

It was close to two o'clock as they neared Tunis, and as they approached the airport, Liam's cell rang. He grabbed it, hoping the call was from Ullyanov, and was disappointed to see it was only from Joey Sheridan.

"You talk," Liam said, passing the phone to Aidan. He was still irritated Joey had picked this time to show up, and worried he would only make a confusing situation more complicated.

Aidan arranged a pick-up spot with Joey, then hung up. "You're okay with this, aren't you?" he asked.

"No. We're in the middle of an operation. It's a bad idea to insert Joey into the mix."

"That's not all, is it?" Aidan twisted sideways in his seat to face Liam. "You're still freaked out about Joey knowing you're gay."

Liam gripped the wheel. "Will you get off that? Joey's known about me for years."

"Yeah, but there's a difference, isn't there? Between him knowing you're gay and him seeing you with me. Coming to our house."

"I'll deal with it, Aidan." He was about to say something else, asking Aidan to try and be less gay with Joey around—but he realized what a stupid move that would be and shut his mouth again.

He spotted Joey outside the terminal, and despite all his reservations, he was happy to see him. Joey looked the same: broad shoulders, close-cropped black hair, wide smile. Liam wondered if he had changed in the years since he left the SEALs; his hair was longer, for one thing, and he never would have been able to pierce his nipples in the navy.

"Nice ride, buddy." Joey tossed his duffel into the backseat and climbed in after it.

"Rental," Liam said.

Aidan turned and stuck his hand out to Joey. "Welcome to Tunis."

"Good to be here." He released Aidan's hand and sat back against the seat. "So tell me what we're up against."

Liam started to talk but a cab cut in front of him, and he blasted the horn and shouted out the window in Arabic. "You haven't changed a bit, Billy," Joey said, laughing.

"You drive; I'll talk," Aidan said. He gave Joey a quick rundown on the situation.

"So you have nothing," Joey said when he was finished.

"We know the name of the kidnapper, and we have a rough idea of what's at stake," Aidan said. "That's not nothing."

"In SEAL terms, it is," Joey said.

"Yeah, Joey's right," Liam said as he pulled up in front of the little house behind the Bar Mamounia so they could unload their gear. Hayam started barking as they dropped bags on the front stoop, and Aidan opened the door so she could rush out and greet them, then pee on the scraggly tree next door.

"Who's this little sweetheart?" Joey said as she scurried back and sniffed his feet.

"Her name is Hayam," Liam said, starting to ferry bags inside as Aidan drove away to find a parking space for the SUV.

"So you're doing the domestic thing," Joey said, dragging his own duffel and two of Liam's into the living room. "Sweet."

"This isn't weird for you at all?" Liam asked, dropping his bags on the sofa. "I mean, being here, with me and Aidan?"

"Why would it?" Joey asked. "You're my friend. My best friend."

"Yeah, but…"

"I had a feeling you were gay at least a year or two before you came out," Joey said. He stretched his shoulders back, then bent down and touched his toes. "I didn't want to say anything."

"You did? How?"

"I didn't think you were, you know, girly or anything. Just that you never seemed to want to get laid. You never had a date; you never talked about a girl back home." He crossed his arms. "It did piss me off that you didn't say anything, and that I wasn't even the first guy you came out to. But I figured it was all the military crap, the Don't Ask, Don't Tell shit."

Liam was about to respond when Aidan came in. "I'm going to get online," he said. "See if I can find out anything more about this mysterious deal Bazarov's into." He looked at Liam. "You're twitchy as a rabbit. Why don't you work out for a while? Get rid of some of that excess energy so you can focus."

"Yes, sir." Liam saluted Aidan. "Whatever you say, sir."

"That's the attitude," Aidan said as Joey laughed.

"I bet I can still do more push-ups than you can," Joey said. "Especially now that you're living the good life."

"You're on, bud." Without thinking, Liam pulled off his T-shirt and kicked off his shoes, staying in his cargo shorts. While Aidan set up the laptop, Joey stripped down to a pair of white briefs. He dug a pair of tight nylon shorts from his duffel and put them on, then stood and stretched.

Liam forced himself to look away. Would Joey feel comfortable working out with him? Did Joey think Liam would be looking at his body?

Joey didn't seem to care. "Where do we work out around here?" he asked.

"The courtyard." Liam opened the French doors and led Joey outside. They began with warm-ups, then paced each other through sit-ups, push-ups, jumping jacks, and skipping rope. Liam's insecurities slipped away as Joey pushed him to perform.

"That all you've got?" Joey said when Liam had finished a hundred push-ups. Joey switched to one-handed ones and did fifty, Liam following his lead.

He couldn't work out so hard with Aidan; though Aidan had been building his body and his strength during the year they'd been together, his limits were far below Liam's. With Joey, though, he could go as far as he wanted, push through his own pain and exhaustion.

When they finished, an hour or more later, both of them were dripping with sweat, their faces red, their limbs loose as jelly. "That your shower over there?" Joey said, pointing to the wooden enclosure.

"Yeah. I'll get some towels," Liam said.

He looked back as he crossed the courtyard, saw Joey's shorts flung up on top of the wall, heard the water begin cascading. He swallowed and licked his lips nervously, then went inside.

Aidan had put away all the gear and was back at the computer. "Find anything good?" Liam asked him.

Aidan shook his head. "Nothing on Dvorkin, nothing more on this pipeline deal. I put out some feelers, but I haven't gotten anything back."

"Since we have no leads on Maks and nothing else we can do to look for him, we might as well take Joey out to dinner somewhere, show him around, while we can," Liam said. "I'm gonna take a shower; then we'll go."

Aidan nodded and went back to the computer.

Liam went into the bedroom and returned with a pair of oversize towels.

"He seems like a great guy," Aidan said. "I'm glad he's here."

"Yeah. I am too."

Liam stepped out into the courtyard as Joey opened the door of the shower enclosure, then pushed his hands back over his head to smooth his wet hair. Liam handed him one of the towels, allowing himself a quick glance at Joey's body. Funny, but Joey was too muscular for his taste, too bulky—too much like himself. He preferred Aidan's slim physique.

When he finished his own shower, he wrapped the towel around his waist and walked into the living room, where Joey, wearing khaki slacks and a navy polo shirt, was laughing with Aidan and telling him embarrassing stories about Liam's adventures as a SEAL. "I've got a few stories about you, bud," Liam said. "Keep it up and Aidan's going to hear everything about you and the garbage truck in Beirut."

"Bring it on, Billy," Joey said. "I can take it."

Liam went into the bedroom, where he pulled on a pair of lightweight cotton slacks and a button-down shirt in blue and white stripes. He stood at the mirror, inspecting his face for sun damage, wrinkles, and stray hairs, and when he realized how vain he was being, he pulled away. Nobody but Aidan would care how he looked. But he did spray some of Aidan's mousse on his hair and massaged it in.

When he was satisfied with the way he looked, he retrieved Aidan and Joey and they drove down to a seafood restaurant along the waterfront. They shared a bottle of wine and some crisp bread and dined on grilled fish that had been swimming in the Mediterranean that morning.

Liam and Joey laughed and told stories about past operations, and Liam was pleased to see that his old friend and his partner were getting along so well. They all drank more than they should, though Liam could see that Aidan was staying sober enough to drive them back home.

It was late by the time they returned to the little house. Liam took Hayam outside, and when he came back in, Joey was getting ready to camp on the living-room carpet, with a couple of big pillows from the sofa. "Wish we had something more to offer you," Liam said.

"I'm good. You know me. I can fall asleep on concrete, sand—whatever you've got. A nice rug and some fluffy pillows are a treat." He held up his music player, with the earphones dangling from it. "And I've got my tunes, so you guys can get your groove on and I won't hear a thing. I've heard you humping your bunk, and I know you get a little noisy."

Liam could feel his face turning red. "You don't have to worry about that." Across the room, he saw Aidan smiling.

"Shit, I'd worry if you weren't fucking like bunnies," Joey said. "You've got years to make up for, bud. Grab whatever you can."

"Good night," Liam said.

He stalked into the bedroom, Aidan behind him. "He heard you humping your bunk?" Aidan asked.

"You know Joey. He's full of shit."

"But he is our guest." Aidan ran his hand down Liam's arm. "And we should do what he wants."

Liam didn't usually get drunk, but he'd let loose that night, and he could feel his inhibitions slipping away as he took Aidan by the waist and pulled him close. "You think?" he said, bending his head into Aidan's neck, where he nibbled at his lover's earlobe.

He felt Aidan's body tense beneath him. "Oh yeah," Aidan said, pressing his body against Liam's. Liam could feel Aidan's hard-on through his shorts, and he rubbed his thigh against it. He pulled his own shirt off over his head, then unbuttoned his shorts and dropped them to the floor. He kicked off his sandals and stood there in his jockstrap as Aidan hurriedly shucked his own clothes.

Aidan's hands were trembling with desire, and he couldn't seem to find the clasp of his shorts. Liam grabbed the waist and pulled hard, and they went to the floor with Aidan's boxers. Aidan yelped as the fabric caught his stiff dick on the way down.

"Sorry," Liam said, leaning down once more to kiss Aidan's chin.

"No, you're not." Aidan reached around behind Liam and stuck his index finger around the jockstrap and up into Liam's ass. The assault surprised him, and he nearly mimicked Aidan's yelp.

"That's the way you want to play it, huh?" Liam pushed Aidan back and locked his teeth around one of Aidan's nipples.

Aidan moaned, a combination of pain and pleasure, as he drove his finger up Liam's ass again.

Liam ran his hands over Aidan's arms, feeling the silky hair there, pressing Aidan's chest against his own. Just as Aidan loved Liam's muscles, Liam loved the fact that Aidan's body was hairy—his arms, his chest, his groin, even a strip of fine hairs that protected his sweet asshole.

They rubbed their bodies against each other, Liam's dick stiff and poking its head out of his jockstrap. "I want to fuck you, baby," Liam whispered into Aidan's ear, his tongue tracing its curl. "I want to fuck you so hard you'll always remember this night."

It was funny the way Aidan almost wilted in his arms, falling backward to the bed and then turning over, presenting his ass doggy-style.

For a moment, Liam thought of Joey out there in the living room. Was he hearing anything? Imagining anything? Liam had always thought his buddy was one hundred percent straight, but you never knew. The thought excited him even more, and he pulled aside the jockstrap's pouch and grabbed a jar of lube from the bedside table.

He stroked his dick, noting the way the shaft of moonlight from the courtyard played over the floor, the bed, and Aidan's waiting ass. When his dick was slippery, he stepped over to the bed and pulled Aidan's legs toward him. The bed was low, so Aidan ended up at a forty-five-degree angle. Liam grabbed Aidan's hips and positioned his dick at the entrance to Aidan's winking hole.

Then he slammed his dick home. Aidan howled in pain, and that spurred Liam on even further, the alcohol and his thoughts of Joey releasing all his inhibitions. He pounded his dick up Aidan's ass, wondering what would happen if Joey were to come to the door of the bedroom, open it, stand there naked and hard himself.

Would he wait for an invitation? Or just jump into the fun? Would he want to suck Liam's dick? Eat his ass or fuck him? Liam loved Aidan, believed in monogamy—but at that moment if his best buddy had wanted to join the fuckfest, he'd have welcomed him with open arms and open ass.

Aidan was squirming on the bed, whimpering and moaning, his sweat dripping down his back to the crack of his ass where it met with Liam's dick sliding in and out.

Liam had had some fantastic sex since he'd met Aidan—times when his whole body shook with the power of his orgasm. This had to be one of the best. Tears leaked out of his eyes, and he felt like he had lost all control of his body as the orgasm welled up inside him. He reached forward and grabbed Aidan's stiff dick and started jerking it with his sweaty hand, and as he felt Aidan's dick swell up, heard Aidan make those whimpering noises he always made as he was about to come, he lost it completely.

His dick spurted up Aidan's ass as Aidan came in Liam's hand. It was so amazing it was almost painful—he couldn't bear the sensation of his dick against the walls of Aidan's ass, but he couldn't even think of pulling out until every drop of cum had been ejected.

Aidan pushed his hands forward on the bed, sliding until he was lying flat, and Liam went with him, his dick still wedged in Aidan's ass, so painful and yet so amazing. The sweat from his chest mingled with the sweat that had attached to the silky hairs of Aidan's back, and he rested his whole body on top of Aidan's.

He knew Aidan loved that, having Liam's full weight on him, but he knew, too, that he couldn't do it for long. He was just too big and too heavy, and Aidan needed to breathe sometime. So with reluctance he slid his dick out of Aidan's ass and flopped next to him on the bed.

"I sure as hell hope Joey likes his music loud," Aidan said, laughing, as Liam snuggled next to him. "Because I think they probably heard us in the Bar Mamounia."

"Yeah." Liam kissed Aidan's forehead. "So what if they did? Let 'em all know how much I love you."

"Yeah, but I love you more," Aidan said, running his hand over Liam's smooth chest.

Liam smiled and yawned once, and then before he knew it, he was asleep.

Slaughterhouse

The next morning, Liam's dick was still sensitive and his brain was fuzzy. He hadn't drunk that much in a very long time. "Must be getting old," he said to his reflection in the bathroom mirror. Jesus, that was a horrifying thought. Someday his body would betray him, his muscles atrophying, his joints aching.

When he came out of the bathroom, Aidan was already in the kitchen preparing breakfast. While they were eating, Liam's cell rang. "Hello, Faisal. I'm glad to see you're working on a Sunday morning. Do you have anything for me?"

He motioned to Aidan, who had already pulled out a pad and a pen. "I have an address," Faisal said. He read it out slowly, and Aidan copied it down. "I am not sure it is current, but it is the best I can find at present." He paused. "If you discover anything I can use to arrest Khan, you will let me know?"

"Of course."

"I spoke with a lieutenant in the Bizerte police," Faisal said. "Apparently they received a confused story about this incident from the woman in charge. She assured them that it was all under control and that they did not need to investigate. Is that true?"

"If Khan is involved, you know we are dealing with a very sophisticated operative," Liam said. "Do you think the Bizerte police can do anything to help?"

Faisal laughed harshly. "Do not make me speak badly of Tunisian police."

"I may need your help again," Liam said. "I'll be in touch."

He hung up and looked at Aidan and Joey. "We're going to see this guy Rajif Khan. Maybe he can tell us where Murat Dvorkin has the kid stashed."

"You have anything resembling a plan?" Joey said. "Or is this a standard Billy deal? Just blast into the place and twist the guy's nuts until he talks?"

"Is that your standard deal?" Aidan asked, looking at Liam with a smile dancing on his lips.

"Joey's talking metaphorically."

"Yeah, I'm a real metaphorical kind of guy." Joey put his hands behind his head and stretched his legs. Liam forced himself to glance away, worried Joey would catch him looking too interested.

"Do we have a plan?" Aidan asked.

"We're going to scout out the area. Recon is always a good way to start."

"Jesus, you sound just like Hardwick," Joey said, referring to the leader of their SEAL team.

"Hey, I learned some shit. You should try it sometime."

Joey reached over and smacked Liam on the side of the head. "Missed you, bud."

They retrieved the SUV from its parking space, and Liam drove them out the Boulevard du 7

Novembre 1987 toward the Hippodrome de Kaar Said, the horse-racing stadium on the city's east side. The address Faisal had given them was in a run-down neighborhood near the stadium.

After making some twists and turns and getting lost at least once, putting up with verbal abuse from both Aidan and Joey, Liam turned down a narrow side street and slowed the car. "The address Faisal gave us is just ahead. That house with the blue door and the grills on the windows."

The single-story house looked like every other on the street, with a flat tin roof and paint peeling on the stucco walls. It was separated on one side from its neighbor by a narrow alley. There was no way to tell from the outside if anyone was at home.

They circled slowly around the block and then pulled into a parking space that gave them a view of the house's front door. "You both stay here," Liam said. "I'm going to take a closer look." He shifted the SUV into park but left it running. He pulled on his sunglasses and grabbed a red chechia—the round cap many Tunisian men wore—as he stepped outside.

It was hot. Much hotter than it had been in Bizerte, where the Mediterranean provided cooling breezes. It didn't help that he was standing in full sunlight, either.

He crossed the street to where the buildings offered some meager shade. A scrawny dog nosed the side of a building ahead of him, and he could hear kids playing down the block. The rest of the street slumbered in the hot morning.

He walked past the address they had for Rajif Khan, not stopping but all senses on alert. The windows were closed and shuttered, but he heard the hum of a window air conditioner coming from the narrow alley between the house and its neighbor.

At the end of the block, he turned right, sweat beginning to trickle down his forehead and under his arms. He looked around, saw no one watching him, and slipped into the narrow alley that ran behind the houses, with a couple of bicycles and a trash can leaning up against back walls.

Counting the houses, he moved down the street until he was behind Khan's house. The air conditioner dripped water in a rusty stain down the back wall. It filled the only window, and the noise prevented him from hearing anything from inside.

He heard the front door opening and slid up against the wall of the neighboring house. Two men stepped out the door, though from his angle he couldn't see their faces. One clapped the other on the back and said something Liam couldn't hear, then went back inside. The other turned onto the street and walked away.

Liam was frustrated. Who was in the house, and who had left? He slunk forward, between the two houses. The smell of cumin and burned bread wafted from the house next door, so strong that it almost made him want to gag.

He was about halfway down the narrow alley— stepping carefully to avoid the trail of dirty water in the center and the crumpled papers stacked up against one wall—when he saw the SUV move past on the street.

"What the fuck?" he said under his breath. Someone must be on the move. Was it Khan? He ran the rest of the way down the alley, seeing the SUV almost at the corner, and sped ahead.

The back passenger door opened as he got close, and Joey reached out and grabbed the collar of his shirt and pulled as Liam leaped into the moving vehicle.

"Got him," Joey said as Liam sprawled on the seat, the door still open behind him. His head was uncomfortably near Joey's crotch. Well, uncomfortable for him. Why did he have the desire, in the middle of everything that was going on, to sniff Joey's pouch, lick his tongue up the outside of his shorts. God, he had to stop that thinking.

Aidan stepped on the gas and turned the corner fast, Liam sliding backward and almost flying out the door. He grabbed the handle and shut it, pulling a burst of hot air in with it.

"What's going on?" he said, struggling to get up until Joey grabbed the back of his shirt and heaved him up onto the backseat.

"The guy on the motorcycle," Aidan said, pointing ahead. "He's the one who helped Dvorkin grab Maks."

His body was right next to Joey's, their legs entwined. "You're sure?"

"Not a hundred percent. But Joey and I thought following him was worth the gamble."

Liam sat back against the seat, pulling his legs away from Joey's. "You see what I have to put up with?" he asked Joey.

"Hey, what we do for love."

"OMG, he's quoting from *A Chorus Line*," Aidan said. "Maybe you weren't the only gay SEAL on your team after all, Liam."

Joey threw his head back and laughed. "Sorry to disappoint you, bud. I just happen to like musical theater."

"Yeah. I've known guys like that."

"Aidan," Liam said. "Ease up."

"We're just having fun here, Billy," Joey said.

Liam couldn't help the irritation bubbling up. Aidan and Joey were taking over the operation, and he didn't like it one bit. "My name is Liam, all right?"

"No, your name is William Joseph Augustine McCullough," Joey said. "You just started calling yourself Liam when you left the SEALs."

"Augustine?" Aidan said, twisting around. "Is that your confirmation name? You told me you wrote a paper on him when you were a kid. You didn't tell me you took his name too. How old were you when you took that name?"

"Seven. Pay attention to the road. You're following somebody, remember?"

Aidan turned back "I remember. Your parents let you get away with choosing the patron saint of brewers?"

Liam shifted uncomfortably on his seat. "It was about my dad, all right? I told you he was a drunk. I thought maybe if St. Augustine was my patron saint he could help my dad stop drinking."

"And did he?"

Liam laughed harshly. "No. But by the time I figured that out, I was stuck with the name." He leaned forward. "Are you watching that motorcycle? Because it looks like he's about to turn, and you're in the wrong lane to follow him."

"Shit," Aidan said, turning the wheel sharply as the cycle made a couple of quick turns. They found themselves on the Avenue d'Oran, which led west back toward the city center. Aidan kept a safe distance behind the biker, who didn't seem to realize he was being followed.

Liam's cell rang. "It's Ullyanov," he said before he answered. He slid the phone unlocked to answer the call.

"Mr. Bazarov received a phone call," Ullyanov said. "From men who have the boy. They wish Mr. Bazarov to sign a contract that is not in his favor."

"We know who took Maks. Do you recognize the name Murat Dvorkin?"

There was a pause on the line. Liam thought for a moment the call had dropped, but then Ullyanov said, "This is not good. This man is very dangerous. He was part of the old KGB."

"We have his name and his picture, but that's all we've been able to find so far. He's very good at keeping a low profile."

"He is a professional," Ullyanov said. "But that is good for us. He will not kill Maks unless he is paid to do so."

"We're following a lead right now. I will do everything I possibly can to bring Maks back safely."

"I see now we should have given you more information from the beginning," Ullyanov said. "But we did not know that this man Dvorkin was involved. We think it is just contract negotiation, and we are being careful."

"What is the contract for?"

"New pipeline to be built through Turkmenistan for transport of natural gas. It is government contract, but Maximum Gaz will be primary supplier, so government wishes Mr. Bazarov to make recommendation. Russian company has bid, and so has Chinese company. Chinese bid provides Mr. Bazarov with some ownership of the pipeline. Also Chinese company is more trustworthy as business partner."

Ullyanov sighed. "Mr. Bazarov is on his way back to Ashgabat now. Tomorrow he must make his recommendation to the government to sign with Russian company, or message says Maks will die."

"What if Bazarov signs the contract?" Liam asked. "Will the kidnapper release Maks?"

"That is not clear. Mr. Bazarov fears that this Russian company will hold Maks for some time to ensure his cooperation."

"I'll call you when I have more information," Liam said and ended the call.

The motorcyclist slowed and pulled into a parking space. Aidan was a few cars behind, and he came to a stop. "Aidan, stay with the vehicle," Liam said. "Monitor the radio. Joey, you're with me. Let's see where this guy is going."

They fell easily into old patterns. Joey crossed the street and strolled past a row of stores, while Liam put on his chechia once more, slumped his shoulders so he would not appear so much taller than anyone else, and focused on following the subject.

The man stopped at the door to a two-story building with a row of clerestory windows just below the roofline. He rapped on the door, it opened, and he stepped through. Then the door slammed closed behind him. There was a quick beep that signaled an alarm system being engaged.

Liam pointed Joey to the left and went to the right himself, walking through an empty lot beside the building, littered with broken glass and other rubbish. There were no windows at all on that side, and the concrete wall was painted with all kinds of graffiti.

He met up with Joey at the rear of the building, where a faded sign on the back wall announced it had once been a slaughterhouse. Liam thought it still smelled faintly of blood and death. Below the sign were a pair of roll-up doors with heavy metal chains and padlocks keeping them shut. A narrow alley ran along the back side of the building.

"You think the boy is inside?" Joey asked.

"All we can do is wait and watch. See who comes and goes, what kind of food and drink they take in."

"I may have a better idea," Joey said. "You heard about the Eagle series of sensors?"

"Not sure. What are they?"

"Handheld gadgets that use low-power, ultrawideband radio waves to show what's behind walls."

"So we could see if Maks is in there?"

They turned to walk back to the SUV. "Not that precise. The unit can look through walls of up to twenty centimeters of concrete, but it just shows motion of people or animals. Comes with a controller that looks like you could use it to play video games, and you can display the image on a laptop too."

"You know where you can get your hands on one of these?" Liam asked.

"I need to make a couple of calls. I'll know in an hour or two."

When they reached the SUV, Aidan asked, "Did you find Maks?"

"Not sure. I need to do some more recon."

Liam left Joey at the SUV making his calls and returned to the former slaughterhouse. He had to admit, he couldn't have picked a better location to hold a hostage himself. The only windows were those second-story ones, and there was no way to reach them without leaning a ladder up against the building in plain sight.

The building fronted on a four-lane street with constant traffic. The empty lot was on the right, the alley along the back. The only positive note was a two-story apartment building on the left side, which was close enough that perhaps Liam could jump from one rooftop to the other.

The apartment building was in the old-fashioned style, with a wrought-iron gate that led to a central courtyard. He picked the lock on the gate easily and walked into the dark, musty hallway that led to the courtyard, turning to the left just before he reached it to climb to the second floor.

A fat woman in an abaya, a long, robelike dress, looked out of an open doorway on the second floor. He had a flash of inspiration. There were always vacancies in buildings like this, poor people moving in and out. "Is there an apartment for rent on this floor?" he asked the woman in Arabic.

She just stared at him. He was about to ask again when a small boy appeared from behind her voluminous cloak and said, "It's number six, at the end. Are you going to move there?"

"I don't know yet," Liam answered. "Thanks."

He walked to number six and tried the door. It swung open, and he stepped inside. It was only a single room, with a rudimentary sink along one wall, a counter and a couple of cabinets, and a toilet in a closet.

He left the apartment and walked to the door at the end of the hall. As he hoped, it led to a narrow staircase to the roof. He looked behind him and saw the small boy watching from his doorway. Liam smiled and waved, then stepped into the stairwell.

With the door closed behind him, the stairway was almost impenetrably dark. He waited a minute for his eyes to get accustomed to the darkness and began to climb, testing each step with his foot before putting his weight on it. It was a slow, laborious process, and the heat in the stairwell was insufferable. He sweated freely, wiping his forehead often.

The door to the roof was rusted shut, and Liam couldn't see how to force it open. He turned to go back downstairs when the second-floor door opened, flooding the stairwell with light. Liam froze where he was. Was it the boy, following him? Or the man from the motorcycle?

"Billy? You up there?"

"Yeah, Joey." Liam descended the stairs quickly. "How'd you find me?"

"I can analyze a situation just as well as you can," Joey said as they both stepped into the hallway. "I figured this was the best place to access the building next door."

"We don't even know if it's the right place yet."

"Aidan researched the building's ownership. Belongs to a company that he tracked back to your guy Rajif Khan."

"Yeah, that makes sense, because we tracked the motorcycle from Khan's. This could be a completely different operation. Can you get us that sensor device?"

"Waiting for a call."

Liam led Joey to apartment six. "This one's vacant," he said, opening the door. "If we need a base, we can use it."

Joey walked inside and went to the window. "Clear view of the front door. That'll help with surveillance." He sat down on the floor and leaned against the wall, his eyes on the front door of the slaughterhouse. "I'll take the first watch. You guys get everything set up."

"Will do," Liam said.

He was at the door when Joey said, "You got yourself a sharp boy there. Make sure you don't let him slip away."

"I'll take that under advisement," Liam said and closed the door behind him.

Tightrope

Liam returned to the SUV, where Aidan had hooked up the air card to the laptop so he could surf from the phone's signal. Liam began pulling bags from the back of the SUV. "We don't know for sure that the boy's inside, but it's our best guess," he said. "I found a temporary HQ in that building, and Joey's monitoring the situation. Let's get our gear up there."

They locked the SUV and humped the duffels down the block to the apartment building, where Liam led the way to the second floor. "First order of business is to get access to the roof," he said, dropping his bag to the ground. He knelt down next to it and found a high-powered flashlight, a set of lock picks, and a spray bottle of machine lubricant, and added that to the Swiss Army knife in his pocket.

He went back out into the hallway, where the same little boy was watching from his own doorway. Liam had never been much good with kids, and he'd been away from his own family for so long he had no exposure to his nieces and nephews. He smiled at the kid, though, and the kid smiled back.

The stairs were much easier to climb with light, and at the rooftop landing, he played the flashlight around the door frame looking for the problem. The old metal door had warped in the frame, and though he was able to get the lock open easily, the door still wouldn't budge. He popped the hinges and used one of the knife blades to pry the door away from the frame on that side. He was able to get it open enough that he could slide through. He found a piece of wood on the roof and used that to keep the door from swinging shut.

The tar-paper roof was roasting hot, even through the soles of his sandals. He had a good view of the roof next door, where there were four industrial-size fans. All were silent. The two buildings were close enough that he could swing a board from one roof to the other and walk across.

The apartment building was located in La Manouba, in the middle of the semicircular ring of suburbs around the old city of Tunis, and from the roof he had a panoramic view of the skyline. To the east he could see the square tower of the Zitouna mosque towering over the souk in the heart of the medina. Surrounding it were what passed for high-rise office buildings, and the glassy rectangular block of the Hotel Africa.

A line of tall palms framed the P7 highway that led back to the city, and a load swung from a construction crane on the edge of downtown. In the distance were the Sidi Bel Hassen hills, blue-gray in the morning light, and he thought he could just make out sunlight glinting off the Lac de Tunis.

The area had been inhabited, he knew, for nearly three thousand years, and seeing the city like that always made him stop to think about how tiny he and everyone he knew was, within that grand scope of time.

But even so, a boy was missing and it was his responsibility to find him and bring him home.

He wiped the sweat from his forehead and climbed back downstairs.

Aidan was sitting on the floor across from Joey, writing out a list of items they needed. "The power's out," he said. "We're going to need to recharge our phones and cameras, so I want to pick up our little generator." It wasn't big enough to run appliances, but it would do for small equipment. "We're also going to need some food and bedding and toilet paper."

"All the comforts of home," Joey said. He looked back outside and said, "Hello. We've got action at the front door."

He picked up the digital camera, zoomed it, and started taking pictures as Liam and Aidan joined him at the window. A man was standing at the front door, waiting for it to be opened. "That looks like Dvorkin," Aidan said.

The man entered the building, the door shutting behind him. They heard the alarm system beep again. Joey turned the camera's screen to them and zoomed in on the face of the man as he waited for the door to open.

"Yup, that's him," Liam said. "Scar matches. So that means it's a better than average chance that Maks is inside."

Joey's cell phone rang. He flipped it open and turned away from them to speak in a low voice.

Liam was annoyed. What was Joey saying that he and Aidan couldn't hear? But then his old training kicked in. Everything in an op had to be on a need-to-know basis. You shared what you could, or had to, with your teammates, but you were always careful with how information was spread.

Joey disconnected his call and turned back to them. "I've got to pick up the device. Somebody who knows this city want to drive me?"

"I'll do it," Liam said. "I'm going to need some other supplies anyway."

Aidan scrawled a few more items on his list and handed it to Liam. "Bring me some takeout on your way back." He took over Joey's position at the window.

The little boy was hovering in his doorway, and Liam ruffled his hair as they walked past. The boy smiled shyly and lowered his head, then turned back into the apartment.

"Just like old times, huh, bro?" Joey said as they walked down the narrow staircase. "You ever miss those days?"

"All the time." They exited the dark stairs to the brilliant light of the courtyard. "But you move on, you know? How about you? You ready to go back to civilian life?"

"Nah, not for a while yet. I'm still having too much fun." When they got to the SUV, he said, "You know where the embassy is?"

"That's where you're picking up this device?"

"You remember Louie Fleck?"

"Yeah, he's a friend these days," Liam said. "I should have thought to call him myself. The CIA gets all the good toys."

Fleck was gay too, with a Tunisian boyfriend, and he and Aidan had dinner with them sometimes. But it wasn't up to him to out Fleck to Joey. Fleck was CIA, though his official job title was cultural liaison. Liam knew Fleck was comfortable in the closet.

"Actually he's just procuring it for me," Joey said. "I don't know exactly where it's coming from, and I don't want to know."

"Works for me."

Liam had a reasonably good map of Tunis in his head, so he quickly found his way back to the P7 and drove into the center of the city. He pulled up outside the embassy and said, "There's a hardware store down the street. I'm going to do some quick shopping and then come back for you."

"Roger that." Joey hopped out and showed his ID to the guard at the gate as Liam pulled away.

At the hardware store, Liam bought a range of supplies, including two boards long enough to span the gap between the apartment building and the slaughterhouse. The boards were too long to fit inside the SUV, so he had to position them through the rear window. He never liked open windows in a vehicle during an operation; it was too easy for the bad guys to get access to you. But it would have to do.

When he returned to the embassy, Joey was standing at the gate with a small duffel bag, talking to the guard. He swung into the front seat, carrying the duffel with him. "Got what you needed?" Liam asked.

"Yup. Louie wasn't happy about having to come to work on a Sunday, but that's life. He dropped in a few other toys we might be able to use, including a tranquilizer gun and some M99."

"He just happened to have that handy?" M99 was another name for etorpine, a synthetic opiate used to tranquilize large animals.

"You know Louie. He's got his fingers in a lot of pies, and that comes with a lot of different kinds of pie filling."

"Yeah, that Louie. He's a hell of a baker."

They swung past a small grocery. "You want to shop or you want me to?" Liam asked. "Since we can't lock up, one of us is going to have to stay with the car."

Joey leaned back in his seat. "Don't forget the toilet paper."

"Getting soft in your old age?" Liam teased.

"Hey, I can pop a squat wherever I need to and wipe up with a piece of newspaper. I'm just thinking of your tender civilian butt."

Liam chose not to pursue that line of conversation. The idea that Joey was thinking of his tender butt at all made him uncomfortable, especially considering his own fantasies. Best not to go down that road at all.

Aidan's list was long, and it took him a while to grab everything on it. He finished by ordering three sandwiches and a half dozen big bottles of water. When he got back to the SUV, Joey's eyes were closed, and Liam tried to sneak up behind him.

"Won't work, bud," Joey drawled, his eyes still closed. "I can still get the drop on you."

Liam didn't want to open the back hatch and disturb the boards, so he loaded the groceries in the backseat. "You haven't changed a bit, have you?"

"Got smarter and better looking. That's about it."

Liam laughed and drove them back to the apartment. Liam took the boards, and Joey loaded up with everything else. When they reached the second floor, Aidan was sitting by the window, his back propped against a couple of duffels. "Make yourself comfortable," Liam said, dropping the boards along one wall.

"The motorcycle guy left, and I got a couple of pictures of him as he walked out. You want to e-mail them to your police buddy, see if he recognizes him?"

"Yes, sir." Liam stretched his arms and flexed his back. The boards weren't heavy, they were just awkward.

"I like that attitude," Aidan said. "Keep it up."

Joey snickered and dropped the food on the countertop. The hardware supplies went on the floor next to the boards; then he replaced Aidan at the window.

"I already transferred the photos to a folder on the hard drive," Aidan said, motioning to the laptop. "I tested the air card, and it works in here. Have you got an e-mail address for Faisal?"

"I've got it under control, Aidan," Liam said grumpily. He sat on the floor with the laptop, and Aidan handed him a sandwich and a bottle of water.

"Done," Liam said after he'd sent the e-mail. He pushed the laptop away from him. "Happy now?"

"You guys sound just like an old married couple," Joey said.

"You know how to work that unit, Sheridan?" Liam asked. "Or do we need to find you an instruction manual?"

Joey looked insulted. "I can figure it out. But let me finish my lunch, will you?"

"Fine. I need to change the lock anyway." He opened one of the bags from the hardware store and pulled out a heavy-duty lock with a dead bolt.

"I'll get the one off the door for you," Aidan said. He picked up a screwdriver and began removing the old lock. By the time Liam had the new lock assembled, Aidan had the old one in pieces on the floor. Aidan cleaned up as Liam slotted the new lock into the door, screwed it in place, and tested each of the keys.

"Are you finished eating yet, Sheridan?" Liam said.

Joey gobbled the rest of his sandwich, grumbling as he did, and then drained half a bottle of water in one gulp. "Ready." He picked up the duffel with the sensor unit inside, and Aidan took his place back at the window.

They went down the stairs in silence, but just before they went outside, Joey stopped and asked, "You aren't pissed at me, are you Bil—Liam?"

"Pissed? Why?"

"You seem to have a stick up your butt most of the time," Joey said. "I don't know if it's me or Aidan."

"It's neither of you. It's a guy named Murat Dvorkin. He skunked me and kidnapped a kid I was supposed to be protecting. It's pissed me off."

"We'll get the kid back."

"Yeah. We will." As Liam pushed the front door open, he thought about what Joey had said. He was mad at Dvorkin, sure, but there was something more, something unsettling about having his past and present lives come together. Joey and Aidan, being a SEAL and being a bodyguard. Being in the closet and being open about his sexuality. But if he expected this operation to succeed, he had to get his emotions under control.

They walked around the slaughterhouse together, looking for a good place to set up. They found a corner where the angle of the apartment building blocked them from the street, but where they could get a clear line on the slaughterhouse wall.

"We may need to try a couple of different angles," Joey said as he started unpacking the gear.

Liam picked up the portable generator that would power the unit and got it working as Joey assembled the sensor. The display unit looked like a handheld video game.

"All right. Let's power this baby up and see what we've got."

The unit went through a series of calibrations, and then the display lit up, identifying two sources of heat inside the building. One lay on the floor, while the other sat on a chair across the room.

"That must be Dvorkin," Joey said, pointing at the display. "And you think that's the kid on the floor?"

"Hard to say. Could just be another accomplice." As they watched, the person on the floor sat up and tried to stretch, but one arm would only go so far.

"Looks like restraints," Joey said.

"Yeah. So let's assume that's Maks. Next question is how we get him out."

"I'm going to play around with this unit for a while," Joey said. "See if I can learn anything about the building."

"Good. I'm going to work on the bridge over to the other building while it's still daylight."

He went back upstairs. "It looks like there's a hostage in there," he said to Aidan. "Can't say for certain it's Maks, but the chances that Dvorkin is running two different kidnap operations is pretty damn slim."

"And?"

"And I'm still working on a plan. I'll be back." Liam grabbed the bag of supplies, then picked up the boards and walked out the door. The little boy was standing in his doorway, and when he saw Liam carrying the two long boards, he scampered down the hall to the stairway door and held it open.

"*Shukran,*" Liam said.

The boy didn't answer, but as soon as Liam was through the door, he ducked under the boards and ran up the stairs. At the roof, he pushed open the door and held it once again.

"You're strong," Liam said in Arabic. "That door is heavy."

The boy didn't say anything, but he did smile and then quickly looked down at the ground. "You want to be my helper?" Liam asked.

"Aywa!" the boy said, nodding eagerly.

Liam dropped the bag of supplies by the door and carried the two boards toward the edge of the roof. "What's your name?"

"Youssef."

"I'm Liam." He held out his hand to the boy, who grasped it. "Nice to meet you."

It was already late afternoon and the sun had dipped behind some big cumulous clouds, so it was cooler on the roof. Liam looked down at the alley between the apartment building and the slaughterhouse and saw Joey bent over the sensor unit.

Liam had always worked best when he was alone, and sometimes Youssef was more trouble than help. But Liam liked having the kid around, and the work went quickly as he built a framework to hold one end of the boards. Youssef brought him nails and held things steady as Liam put together the framework.

"That looks good," he said, leaning back. "Shukran, Youssef."

Youssef smiled shyly.

Liam lifted one of the boards and laid it down from one roof to the other, slotting it into the framework he had built. Then he repeated the process with the other board. "I need you to do something for me, Youssef," he said, leaning down to the boy's level.

"Aywa," Youssef said.

"I need you to stay here and make sure the board stays in the slot." He looked at the boy. "This is a very important job. Can you handle it?"

The boy nodded eagerly.

"Good." He stood up and placed his right foot on the right-hand board. It wobbled just a fraction. He placed his left foot on the left board and stood there for a moment, steadying his breathing.

Slowly, carefully, he walked across the boards. He wasn't sure he had calculated correctly; would there be enough board on the opposite roof to balance his weight? But he refused to worry and focused instead on crossing the space without losing his balance.

Halfway there, the board bowed unexpectedly. Liam nearly lost his balance, but he kept his feet firmly planted on the board, and once it stopped wobbling, he kept going.

When he reached the roof of the slaughterhouse, he heard Youssef clapping. "Ssh!" he said, turning back to the boy with his finger at his lips.

The boy stopped in midclap, looking down at the rooftop again. Liam walked across the slaughterhouse roof, which was much heavier and firmer than the one on the apartment building. The only point of vulnerability seemed to be the industrial-size fans in the center of the roof.

He pulled out his cell phone and took a number of photos, focusing on the fan housing and the nuts and bolts that kept it connected to the roof. The opening was large enough so that if he and Joey could get the housing off, they could drop themselves in and rappel down.

It wasn't much, but it was the start of a plan. He snapped the phone closed and walked back to the bridge. Youssef was standing at the roof's edge, watching him closely. Liam smiled.

He was sweating heavily, and he stopped to pull his shirt off. He used it to wipe his forehead, his head, and under his arms. Then he put it back on, shivering just a moment as the wet fabric plastered itself to his skin, and stepped onto the board.

This time he anticipated the bounce halfway across. He steadied himself, his eyes focused on Youssef, not on the ground below.

As he got to the apartment building, the boy's face split open into a wide grin.

"Good job," Liam said, ruffling the boy's dark hair again. He pulled the boards out of the housing and left them at the edge of the roof. He collected the equipment and ushered Youssef downstairs ahead of him.

"This is our secret, right, Youssef?" he asked. "You aren't going to tell anyone?"

"*La*," the boy said, shaking his head.

"Good boy," Liam said. "Now, back to your mother."

Dossier

Aidan shifted position in front of the window, trying to get comfortable. How did Liam manage? He could fall asleep at the drop of a hat. Aidan never saw him squirm or complain about conditions. Was it all that military training? Or was Liam just some kind of strange creature who was physically and temperamentally suited to thrive in difficult conditions?

He looked out the window again, toward the door of the slaughterhouse. What was going on in there? Was Maks comfortable? The poor kid must be scared out of his wits. If they could all just get back to the monastery, things would be fine again.

Or would they be? He couldn't deny that he felt more comfortable in the classroom than he did out in the world, protecting someone. Though he had been working for a year to learn Arabic, improve his shooting skills, and imitate Liam in every way possible, this new life never seemed to fit him quite as well as his old one did.

"Anything going on?" Joey asked as he walked into the apartment.

"Nothing." Aidan squirmed around again, shifting the position of the bag he was leaning on. "How do you guys do this—sit for hours and watch nothing happening?"

"You train yourself." Joey put the sensor unit down on the counter and stretched. He touched his toes a few times and flexed his back muscles.

Aidan was struck by how perfect Joey's body was. He wasn't as handsome as Liam, but if anything, he was in better shape. His arm muscles rippled beneath the sleeves of his skintight T-shirt, and his legs, stretching out from his nylon running shorts, were finely delineated, even beneath a light coating of dark hair. Joey was a beefy, black-haired guy, with curiously light eyes and a perpetual five o'clock shadow that complemented his strong jawline.

Joey would be a better match for Liam, Aidan thought. They would be an amazing team, able to outwit any opponents. Good thing Joey was straight or Aidan would be out on his ass.

"Want me to take over?" Joey asked.

"Yeah. I've got to run back to the house and pick up some stuff."

Aidan stood up and stretched. He was in his thirties, for Christ's sake. He should be behind a desk in a classroom, not spying on a kidnapper in some hellhole. Was this what he had studied so long for? Worked a series of crappy jobs back in the States to make money, holding out for the distant chance of a full-time teaching job?

"You need anything?" he asked Joey.

"Nah, I'm good." Joey sat down by the window and made himself comfortable on the hard floor.

He found the SUV parked around the corner from the apartment building, jumped in, and turned the air conditioning on full blast. He didn't usually mind the heat, but the inaction in the hot one-room apartment had made him sweaty, and the oppressive heat of the neighborhood so far inland didn't help.

He didn't have the same internal map of Tunis that Liam had, so it took him a few wrong turns and detours to find his way back to the P7 that would take him into downtown. Once he found it, he dialed Madame Abboud's cell phone.

"*Allo, oui?*" she said.

"Madame Abboud? It's Aidan Greene. How are the kids doing?"

"Monsieur Greene! Where are you? Where is Maksat Bazarov?"

"I'm in Tunis. Maks is being held hostage so that his father will sign a business deal, but we have the place under surveillance and we're planning a rescue operation."

"*Mon dieu*! This is so horrible. Not to mention very inconvenient. Such an event could be very harmful to my business. You must retrieve this boy as soon as possible."

Typical Madame Abboud, Aidan thought. Worried more for herself and her business than for a scared teenage boy held hostage in an abandoned slaughterhouse. "How are the other kids taking it?"

"Everyone is very upset. It is all the students talk about. I have already heard from many parents. You will be back at the monastery tomorrow?"

"I can't say for sure," Aidan said.

"But who will teach your classes?"

"I guess you will, Madame."

"Me! I am not a teacher. I am merely a businesswoman."

For some reason, Aidan had always believed Madame Abboud was an ESL teacher herself. But it made sense; she really had no clue how classes were run. "You'll have to get one of the other instructors to cover for me."

"This is most inconvenient."

Aidan resisted the impulse to lash out at her. It wasn't her fault Maks had been kidnapped, and she did have some legitimate complaints. "I'll be in touch," he said and ended the call before she could grumble anymore.

He had been hired to teach, after all. That was his primary responsibility. Should he go back to the monastery, leave the rescue operation to Liam and Joey? They were clearly the ones most capable of handling it. He still had papers to grade and lesson plans to prepare. Six weeks was already too short a time to teach these kids to communicate effectively in English, and every day he missed would make things even harder for them.

Who was his real obligation to? To Madame Abboud, who had hired him and who was paying his salary? To the kids, who needed his help? To Maks, who needed to be rescued? Or to Liam? When he began working with Liam, he had made a commitment to be there, to help him with his business. But more important, to be by his side, no matter what came their way.

It was all so confusing. He parked the SUV a block from the house and walked in the front door, avoiding the bar across the courtyard because he knew Hayam would make a fuss if she spotted him. He was retrieving the portable generator from its place in the back of the closet when he heard a loud rapping on the back door.

Had Mohammed the bartender seen him come in anyway? Or perhaps Abdullah, the pesky boy who was always after Liam. Or had Dvorkin discovered who they were and tracked them down?

He reached for his gun and realized he had taken it off when he was trying to get comfortable by the window and left it at the apartment. What a stupid mistake. Liam would never do something like that. He looked around frantically for something he could use to defend himself in case it was Dvorkin. But Liam had packed up most of their equipment to take with them to Bizerte, and it was all with Liam at the apartment.

Shit, shit, shit. Could he just sneak out the front door, pretend he had never heard the knock? Whoever it was banged on the door again.

He took a deep breath. He was being stupid. The first thing to do was look out into the courtyard and see who was at the door. Then he could figure out what to do next. He slid out of the bedroom, staying close to the wall, until he could get a view out the window to the courtyard. Then he sighed deeply, feeling the adrenaline run down. The dark-skinned Tunisian in the military-style khaki shirt with epaulets was quite familiar to him.

"Faisal," he said, opening the door to the cop. "What are you doing here?"

"I have come to see Liam. Is he here?"

Aidan shook his head. He didn't know how much Liam would want him to say to Faisal. Even though the cop was Liam's friend and had helped him on many occasions, he was still a police officer, and he might try to take over the operation. Bringing the police in at this stage could make things much more difficult.

"Come inside. Liam's out. Can I help you with anything?"

Aidan stepped back so that the Tunisian could enter. Aidan noted his simple black slacks and polished black dress shoes. He was never sure what Faisal's official job was, just that he was some kind of high-ranking official in the national police.

"I have found more information on the man whose photo you sent. He is a petty thief named Mushtaq Oman."

He handed Aidan a couple of pages from a police dossier, and they walked into the kitchen. "Can I offer you some mint tea?" Aidan asked. "Cold water?"

"A glass of cold water would be refreshing."

Aidan poured them both tall glasses from a pitcher in the refrigerator, and they both sat down at the kitchen table.

The dossier contained a picture of the man on the motorcycle and a list of the crimes he had been accused of. "He is a known accomplice of Rajif Khan," Faisal said. "If you can help me arrest Oman, I may be able to use him to get to Khan."

"Right now our first priority is to find and rescue the boy. Khan is secondary."

"To you, perhaps, but not to me. You are involved with some very dangerous men. Khan is one of the most deadly men in Tunisia, and Oman is one of the men he uses to carry out his most violent crimes. And this other man, Dvorkin? If anything, he is more dangerous than both Khan and Oman."

"I understand, Faisal. We'll let you know as soon as we have any information."

"Let it be so." Faisal stood up. "I wish you luck, Aidan. You will need it."

After he let Faisal out of the house Aidan returned to the kitchen table, where he felt his hands shaking. Once again he wondered what he was doing in this situation. Why couldn't he just go back to Bizerte, teach his classes, and leave the dangerous work to Liam?

Visitors

Liam watched as Youssef hurried down the hall to his own apartment, then went into the unit at the far end, making sure to lock and bolt the door from the inside. Joey was at the window. "Where's Aidan?"

"Went home to get some more stuff. What did you see?"

Liam described the fans and their housing. "I'm thinking we rappel down, then shoot the guard with the tranquilizer gun and take the boy out the front door."

"What if the guard has a gun?" Joey said. "He can pick us off as we're dropping."

"We'll just have to be quicker and better shots."

"Normally you mix the M99 for the tranq guns with water," Joey said. "But if we can convert it to an aerosol, we can flood the gas down into the building and knock the guard out. Then we can get in without a problem."

Liam remembered how in 2002, Chechen rebels had taken hostages in a theater. The Russians pumped a gas made of M99 into the building, knocking out the rebels—and the hostages. Over a hundred people had died from the incapacitating effect of the gas. "You mean like the Russians did in Moscow?"

"Yeah, but we've got the antidote," Joey said. "We put on gas masks, rappel down, then we shoot the kid up with naloxone. We give the guard an injection too—after we tie him up."

"I think it could work. We're going to need more supplies, though." He called Aidan's cell. "You still at the house?"

"Yeah. Faisal just came by with a dossier about the guy who's guarding Maks. His name is Mushtaq Oman, and he's not a very nice guy."

"I'll look at the dossier when you get back here. You have a piece of paper? We're going to need some more gear."

He began listing the material Aidan had to bring from the house. "We're going to need rope too. Can you find a hardware store open on Sunday and pick some up? At least fifty feet."

"I'll get on it," Aidan said.

"Good man. Be careful. Love you." As he said the words, which he and Aidan often repeated to each other, he worried what Joey might think. But Joey was busy peering out the window and appeared not to have heard.

He worked on a sketch of the slaughterhouse, trying to figure out the interior from the position of the rooftop fans and what he had been able to see from the sensor's display. As he was finishing, his cell rang, and he noted from the display it was Ullyanov.

"Mr. Bazarov would like to know what is the situation?"

Liam was superstitious about revealing the details of any plan before it was ready to be executed, even to the client. "We're working on a plan. I can't say any more than that right now."

"Whatever is done must be done quickly. Mr. Bazarov is to make his recommendation tomorrow, and then Maks can come home."

"You want him in Ashgabat? Or in Bizerte, to finish his course?"

He heard Ullyanov turn away from the phone and speak in that Turkish-inflected language. When he came back, he said, "We will see when the contract has been signed. Consider that you are still to protect Maks until further notice, wherever he is."

"Will do."

Joey looked up from his position by the window. "What happens after we get the boy? We bring him back here?"

"We can't. This place isn't secure enough. And we can't go back to our house with him, because Dvorkin must know who we are by now. As soon as Aidan gets back, I'll put him onto finding us somewhere to go."

"Works for me." Joey went back to the window, but a moment later, he said, "Hello. Hummer pulling up outside. This doesn't look good."

"What?" Liam scrambled over to the window.

"Those two men, getting out of the Hummer." He handed the binoculars to Liam. "Recognize them?"

"Nope. But it looks like they're coming in here, not the building next door."

Liam pressed the speed dial for Aidan's phone. "Where are you now?"

"Just getting ready to leave the house."

"Stay there until I call you back. We may have a situation here." He closed the connection before Aidan could pester him with questions.

They heard the two men tramping up the stairs, and took positions by the door, their weapons drawn.

The second floor shook as the men stamped down the hall; then one rapped sharply on the door. "Open up," a male voice said in Arabic. "We are from the landlord."

Liam looked at Joey, who nodded. He took up a defensive position behind the door, and Liam holstered his weapon. He left the chain on the door and opened it a fraction. "Aywa?" he asked.

The two men looked like thugs, square-shouldered with a day's growth of beard.

"If you want to live here, you must pay the rent," the first man said. He named a figure in dinars that Liam thought was extortionate, and Liam responded by cutting the number in half.

Joey smiled, poised with his gun out of sight of the men at the door.

The two men conferred, and the first one began to haggle with Liam. When they had achieved a compromise, Liam said, "One minute," and closed the door.

He retrieved his wallet from the bag by the window and pulled out the necessary cash. Then he returned to the door and opened it once again with the chain still on. "I need a receipt," he said, showing the man the cash.

The first man grunted, and the second pulled a receipt book from his pocket. "Name?" he asked.

"Omar Ali," Liam said, picking the most common name he could think of.

The man raised an eyebrow at him but scribbled out the receipt and handed it to him. Liam gave him the cash.

"When you go, leave the keys for the new lock with Mrs. Pashto down the hall," the first man said, and the two of them turned to walk away.

Liam closed the door, then unhooked the chain and looked into the hallway. He saw Youssef sticking his head out his own door, watching the men go. When they had stepped into the stairwell, Liam motioned toward him.

"Did you tell someone we were here?" Liam asked, stepping out into the hall as the boy approached.

Youssef looked down at the ground. "Just my mother," he said in a small voice. "But not about the roof."

"Is your mother Mrs. Pashto?"

The boy nodded.

"You're a good kid, Youssef." Liam pulled a thirty-dinar note from his pocket, the equivalent of about twenty US dollars. "Give this to your mother. Tell her I will give her more when we leave if she doesn't say anything more about us."

Youssef took the note.

"And this is for you," Liam said, handing the boy a five-dinar coin. "For your help this afternoon. I don't think you should tell your mother about it, though."

Youssef smiled broadly. "No, Mr. Liam. You are my friend."

Liam went back inside and called Aidan. "False alarm," he said. "Come back whenever you're ready."

"But what..."

Liam ended the call before Aidan could get his question out.

"You know he's just going to grill you when he gets back," Joey said.

"Yeah, but I'll get you to tell him." He looked at Joey. "And speaking of which, would you mind explaining what the hell you're doing here in Tunis?"

"Can't a guy just drop in to visit a friend?" Joey had resumed his place by the window. Darkness was falling, and he had a pair of night vision binoculars by his side.

"I know you, Sheridan. There's something up. What is it?"

Joey took a long drink from the water bottle next to him. "You remember me telling you about my buddy Phil? From back home?"

"The guy who robbed the liquor store?"

Joey winced. "Yeah, that's him. But he was a good guy when we were kids, you know? He just took a wrong turn."

"More than that," Liam snorted.

"You want me to tell you this story? Then shut up."

Liam sat down on the floor across from Joey, his back against the kitchen counter. There was nothing else to do but wait for Aidan to return with the supplies. "I'm listening."

"Phil was always the kind of guy who'd go along with anything," Joey said. "He'd have joined the navy with me, except he had a heart murmur that kept him out. Once I was gone, he started hanging out with some scumbags we knew from elementary school, and that's how he ended up in jail."

"What does this story have to do with your showing up in Tunis?"

"I'm getting there. Keep your pants on."

Liam got another one of those weird feelings, but he ignored it. "I'm listening."

"I called home a couple of weeks ago, and my mother told me Phil got shanked in the state prison."

"Sorry."

"It really shook me up, you know? I mean, this guy was my best friend growing up, and when I took off for the navy, I kind of left him behind, and look what happened to him."

"He wasn't your responsibility, Joey."

"I know that. But it made me think about you."

Liam laughed. "Don't worry; I'm not planning to hold up any liquor stores."

"Shut the fuck up, all right? You were my best friend in the SEALs, and then you, you know, took a different turn. I didn't want our friendship to end just because of that."

Liam felt his throat closing up, the way it did sometimes when Aidan said something romantic or touching. "Our friendship isn't going anywhere. I may not have said so, but I'm glad you showed up."

"Yeah, well, you know me. I'll go anywhere for a good time, as long as it involves guns and car chases."

"I'll try to accommodate you," Liam said.

Joey picked up the binoculars and looked out the window. "Aidan's pulling up outside. You want to help him or you want window duty?"

"I'll help him." Liam stood up, walked over to Joey, and held his hand out for a fist bump. "Hoo yah, brother."

"Hoo yah," Joey said, knocking his fist against Liam's.

It's a Gas

"You want to play chemist?" Liam asked Joey. "Since this aerosol thing is your idea?"

"Sure." Joey took the M99, a spray gun, and some other equipment, and headed for the toilet stall.

"Take a mask too," Liam said, tossing him one. "I'll keep the naloxone out here."

"Good to know you have such faith in me." Joey caught the mask with his free hand and hung it around his neck.

Liam turned to Aidan. "You're going to have to find us a place to go once we pick up Maks. We can't stay here, and we can't go home."

"One step ahead of you, as usual. I did some searching online before I left the house. I thought we should find a hotel with private villas, but the only hotel I could find that fit the bill was the Golden Sands in La Marsa."

"You do have champagne tastes," Liam said. "But what the hell, Maks's father is paying the bill."

"Nice place?" Joey called back, stepping into the toilet stall.

"One of the nicest," Liam said. "Five stars, right on the beach."

"Sounds like fun." He put the gas mask on his head and ducked into the tiny room. He closed the door behind him.

"You don't think it's too much?" Aidan asked. "It's close to a thousand dollars a night."

Liam shrugged. "If it keeps his son safe, I'm sure it's worth it. But they better have damn good room service at that price."

"We'll try it out tomorrow morning. I have us guaranteed for late arrival tonight."

"Come on, let's get some of this crap stowed so we're ready for a quick departure." While Joey fiddled with the M99, Liam and Aidan loaded everything they wouldn't need for the rescue in the back of the SUV. By the time they came back up to the apartment, Joey said they were ready to roll.

They checked the two-way radios, and then Aidan went down to the street to wait in the SUV. Liam looked up and down the hall to make sure Youssef or his nosy mother wasn't watching, then motioned the all clear to Joey.

He shouldered a coil of rope, and Joey took the gas, and they climbed back to the roof. The darkness was like a presence on the roof with them. There was only the light of a crescent moon, and the occasional reflection of a pair of headlights passing on the street below.

They both attached headlamps to their foreheads and worked swiftly, using only the moonlight and the ambient light that rose from the street. Liam put out the wooden planks again, sliding one end of each into the housing he had built earlier in the day. He stepped on the plank and gingerly moved a foot forward. The plank held under his weight.

"There's a dip halfway across," he said as he inched forward. "Be careful."

It was a lot harder crossing in the dark than it had been in the daylight. He hated to look down, but it was the only way to be sure he was placing his feet correctly. He felt himself sweating again, though the night air was cooler than it had been during the day.

There was so little noise around that he heard as well as felt every movement of the boards. The only other sounds were the occasional car passing below and a distant music, along with the buzzing of a generator somewhere nearby.

He finally made it across, letting out a breath he hadn't realized he was holding. He turned to watch Joey. The bastard had the balance of a cat. Liam shook his head as Joey nearly danced across the boards.

Once they were both on the roof of the slaughterhouse, they sat down at opposite sides of the fan housing. Liam sprayed lubricant on the nuts and bolts on his side, and then handed the can to Joey, who did the same. They worked swiftly, removing the superstructure over one large fan.

Liam shut his headlamp off and peered down through the blades. A man sat at a table, with a small battery-powered flashlight shining as he played solitaire. In the corner, Maks lay on his makeshift bed, curled in the fetal position.

They secured their large rope to the other fan and tested the knots. Joey had rigged a timer on the aerosol spray, and he coiled a rope around it and lowered it carefully between the fan blades. A breeze blew up and caught the unprotected blades, which began to swirl lazily.

Liam slid his right hand into one of the heavy gloves they'd brought for use when shinnying down the rope, then grabbed a blade so the fan would not slice through the rope. He felt the blade press sharply into his hand and hoped the glove's leather would hold.

The detonator on the spray went off, and the can sprayed the paralyzing gas into the large room below. The solitaire player looked up and cursed, then began coughing.

Joey and Liam removed the last bolts from the fan. Liam turned to Joey, offering his upper arm, and Joey injected the antidote. Then he handed a needle to Liam, who injected him. Liam threaded the rope down into the opening and tugged it one last time to make sure it was secure. Then he grabbed the rope in both hands and kicked off into the opening.

The gas was filling the room as he let himself down. Maks was lying on the ground, and his guard had stumbled to the floor and passed out.

Liam reached the floor and hurried over to the guard, whom he recognized as Mushtaq Oman. Joey was just a moment behind him, going to Maks first with the antidote. As Liam began binding Oman's feet, he heard Joey talking to Maks.

"Okay, buddy, I'm just going to stick this needle in your thigh, and then you're going to wake up. Little bit of pain but you won't even feel it."

Liam felt woozy as he tied the knot around Oman's feet. He worried that the antidote wasn't working as well as it should. "Leave the boy for a minute and help me with this guy," he said. He coughed. "Give the antidote a minute to work."

Joey moved Oman to his side on the floor and injected the naloxone into the man's upper arm. Liam bound Oman's arms with a coil of rope, then handed the rope to Joey and went over to Maks.

The teenager was breathing shallowly, but he still wasn't awake. "Come on, Maks, wake up," Liam said, pressing the boy's shoulder. He turned to Joey. "You're sure you mixed the stuff up right?"

His breathing felt increasingly labored. What if Joey had confused the percentages on the aerosol, and they'd given Maks a fatal dose? *Sorry, Mr. Bazarov, we killed your son while rescuing him.*

Maks opened his eyes and began coughing. "That's good," Liam said, clapping him on the back. "Cough it all out." Relief flooded his body, and he coughed a few times himself.

Maks looked around in confusion and tried to struggle against Liam. "It's all right, Maks," he said, helping the boy to his feet. "We're getting you out of here."

"The alarm system is armed," Joey called from the door.

"We'll just have to bust out," Liam said.

Joey flipped the bolt and opened the door as Liam and Maks came up behind him. For a second, all was quiet as they piled out the door. Then a loud siren began.

Aidan was parked in the SUV just outside the slaughterhouse. Joey opened the back door, and the two of them manhandled Maks into the backseat; then Joey scrambled in beside him. Liam hopped into the front seat, and Aidan took off, without even waiting for Liam to close the door.

"You keep doing that," Liam said.

"How much of a head start do you think we have?" Aidan asked.

"Hard to say. Ten minutes at least."

"I swapped the license plates with another SUV I found down the street," Aidan said. "That should confuse them a little."

"Good call."

Aidan threaded his way through the narrow streets. "How are you, Maks?" he called to the backseat.

Maks coughed. "What is happening?"

"You've been rescued," Liam said. "The guy in the back with you is Joey. He's an old friend of mine. The three of us are going to make sure you stay safe."

"Did they hurt you?" Aidan asked. "Do you need anything?"

A car pulled out from a side street, and Aidan leaned on his horn.

"You drive. I'll talk," Liam said. "Maks, are you okay?"

"I am sick at my stomach. I am feeling like I will throw up."

Aidan lowered the window on Maks's side as they reached the Avenue d'Oran, the main street in the area, which would lead them into the center of Tunis. "Out the window, please," he said.

Joey held Maks's shoulders as he leaned out the window and vomited.

It was after midnight, and the city was still awake, with cars and pedestrians at every corner. "Can we stop, please?" Maks said between gasps.

"Sorry," Liam said. "We're in a hurry here. You'll feel better when we get where we're going."

By the time Aidan reached the P9, which would take them out to the seaside suburb of La Marsa, Maks was sitting back against the seat, wiping his mouth with the back of his hand. Joey handed him a water bottle, which he drank from greedily.

Liam opened his cell phone to call Ullyanov and tell him that Maks was safe, but there was no signal. "I'll call when we get to the hotel," he said after three tries.

Aidan pick up speed as they raced past the airport. The road approached the ocean and then turned, and Aidan felt his heart relax a little as the gates of the Golden Sands Hotel appeared ahead. He pulled up at the guard and said, in Arabic, that they had a reservation.

The guard made a face as he smelled the vomit splattered against the side of the SUV, but he asked politely for Aidan's name.

Liam had a bank account and ID in an alias, for use in undercover operations, and Aidan had used that name to make the reservation. Once the guard established that they were expected, he opened the gate and Aidan drove in.

Aidan pulled up at the hotel's porte cochere, and a bellboy approached. Liam hopped out and explained that they were checking into a villa, and the young man led him to the registration desk. He yawned as he handed over the picture ID that matched the name Aidan had registered under, as well as the matching credit card that had guaranteed the room.

While he waited, he tried Ullyanov's phone, but the call went direct to voice mail. "Maks is safe," he said, turning so the concierge did not hear him. "It's very late here, so we'll call you tomorrow with more information."

He ended the call and turned back to the concierge, who ran through four magnetic cards and handed them to Liam in a paper envelope that included a map of the hotel property. "Will you need help with your bags?"

"No, thank you," Liam said and yawned again.

He had to be getting old, he thought as he returned to the SUV. When he'd been in the SEALs, he could have carried out an operation like the one they'd done that evening and still have energy to spare.

He directed Aidan down a winding road through the property until they reached the villa. It was almost two in the morning by then, and all four of them were showing signs of exhaustion. Aidan led Maks inside, where the teen collapsed on the living-room sofa. "I'm going to do a quick recon," he said as Liam and Joey followed him, carrying gear.

Liam felt like he was running on empty as he piled bags against one wall. Even Joey staggered a little as he brought the last bags in.

"Liam and I will take the bedroom on the left," Aidan said. "Joey, you and Maks will be in the second bedroom, over there. I'll take the first watch while you guys get some sleep."

"I should take the first watch," Liam said.

"No, you should get some sleep. You can nod off in about thirty seconds, but I'm too hyped up to sleep right now."

"You won't get any argument from me," Joey said. He turned to the teenager on the sofa. "Come on, Maks. Let's get you tucked in."

He helped the boy up and walked with him to the second bedroom.

"You sure you'll be all right?" Liam asked Aidan.

"You bet. Nobody can trace us here, at least not for a while. There's a coffeemaker in the kitchen in case I start to get sleepy."

"Wake me at six."

"Go to sleep, sweetheart." Aidan leaned up and kissed him on the cheek. "You were amazing tonight."

Liam yawned. "Did you expect anything else?"

Aidan swatted him on the butt and pushed him toward the bedroom. Liam didn't even bother to undress, just fell onto the king-size bed and went to sleep immediately.

Safe Haven

Aidan had so much energy he couldn't sit down. He prowled through the villa, checking windows and doors. It was a single-story building with a flat roof, surrounded by palm trees. The front door opened into a spacious living room with sliding glass doors that led to a patio and an ocean view. The kitchen was to the left, with the guest bedroom to the right. A small foyer at the back right led to the master bedroom, with its own sliding glass doors to the patio.

It wasn't the most defensible property; the sliding glass doors were vulnerable to gunshot, even with the vertical blinds blocking the view. There was a large window from the living room to the front drive, and one from the guest room as well. Both of them had horizontal slatted blinds made of dark wood. The two bathrooms were back to back, between the guest bedroom and the master. The master bath had a window, but the guest bath was surrounded by rooms on each side. A safe room, if it came to that.

He unpacked most of the material from their bags. When he finished that, he walked outside. There were similar villas on each side, each surrounded by palms and spiky aloes. Too many places for a gunman to hide, Aidan thought.

The surf pulsed a few feet away, and the night air smelled of salt and the faintest vestige of coconut tanning oil. The closeness of the Mediterranean was amazing, but it made them vulnerable to attack from the water.

There were a thousand stars overhead, along with the crescent moon. From one of the villas, he heard the low sound of classical music, though he couldn't identify the piece or the composer. Otherwise the only sound was the relentless surf splashing against the shore.

The next day was Monday, and he should be in the classroom at the monastery in Bizerte. It didn't look like that was going to happen, and he'd have to call Madame Abboud again. He did hope that they'd be back maybe by the end of the day, if Bazarov made his recommendation and the threat to Maks was removed.

He had enjoyed the brief return to teaching and wondered what that meant. Was he not cut out for bodyguard work? He loved working with Liam, the physical and intellectual challenges and the adrenaline rush. For the first time in his life, he felt he was in a real partnership. Back in Philadelphia, he'd been with the same man for eleven years, but his life with Blake had always felt more like a job than a love affair.

The bright spot of his life in Philadelphia had been his teaching career and the relationships he established with his students. He loved the act of teaching, of helping someone master the intricacies of the English language. Reading, writing, and speaking were so integral to his own life and his sense of self, and helping a student express him or herself had been very rewarding.

Could he do both? Work with Liam and still teach? Madame Abboud had hired him for a few fill-in jobs, but it wasn't the same as establishing a relationship with a student over a period of weeks or months.

A cool breeze blew up from the Mediterranean. He shivered, rubbed his upper arms, and went back inside, where he made himself a cappuccino, flavoring it with a hot chocolate mix he found in one of the kitchen cabinets. He made a couple of patrols around the outside of the house over the next few hours, and by the time Joey came out of his room just before six, Aidan was ready for bed.

"Anything hopping?" Joey asked, yawning and stretching.

"Nope. Quiet night."

"I'm going to take a quick shower; then I'll take over."

Aidan had been up for nearly twenty-four hours by then, and his battery was almost dead. Joey grabbed his duffel, then disappeared into the guest bathroom. He came out a few minutes later shirtless, in a pair of tight shorts, with his hair wet.

Aidan knew he was tired when the sight of the hunky half-naked SEAL didn't do anything to excite him. His legs felt like lead as he walked the few feet to the bedroom and fell into bed next to Liam, both of them fully clothed.

When Aidan woke, the room was filled with sunlight, and Liam was still asleep next to him. He yawned and looked at the clock. It was almost noon. He stumbled to the bathroom and closed the door quietly behind him.

He washed his face and then looked at himself in the mirror. He was facing his thirty-fifth birthday in the next couple of months, and he could see that the years were starting to take their toll. There were a couple of gray hairs in his beard, and he shaved as soon as he saw them. A couple of lines had etched themselves into his forehead, and it felt like his brown hair was thinning.

Liam was two years older than he was, but still as handsome as ever. What would happen if Liam's looks held but his didn't? What if some handsome guy with a background like Liam's came along? Not Joey Sheridan, who seemed resolutely straight—but there had to be other gay soldiers and SEALs out there.

He looked at his reflection once more, then shrugged. He opened the bathroom door, and as he did, he heard the sounds of muted gunfire coming from the living room. He grabbed his pistol from the bureau top where he'd left it when he unpacked and stepped to the bedroom door. At least this time he knew just where it was. Raising the pistol, he swiveled so he was facing into the living room.

Joey and Maks were sitting on the sofa with video game controllers in their hands. "Gotcha!" Joey said as Maks's on-screen character fell to the ground.

Aidan relaxed, feeling a little foolish and glad that he hadn't burst into the room with his gun out. He returned it to the bureau top, then walked into the living room. "Good to see you've got everything under control out here," he said.

"You look like shit warmed over," Joey said. "Yeah, we're fine. Maks and I are bonding."

"Joey is kicking my ass," Maks said, but he didn't look unhappy.

Aidan laughed and went back into the bedroom. Liam was sitting up and stretching. "Everything okay?"

"Maks and Joey are playing video games."

Liam laughed. "Why am I not surprised Sheridan can bond with a teenager? Did Ullyanov call while we were out?"

Aidan checked Liam's cell and his own. "Nope. I guess we should call for instructions. You sleep all right?"

"Like a baby. How about you?"

"Pretty good." Aidan pulled his polo shirt over his head. "I could use a shower, though." He dropped his shorts and boxers and scratched under one arm. "You interested?"

"I'm interested in getting a little dirtier before we get clean." Liam pulled his own T-shirt off and patted the place next to him on the bed. His gold nipple rings glistened in the bright sunlight.

"What about calling the client?"

"Maks is safe and occupied," Liam said. "If there was any news on their end, they'd have called."

"Good point." As he closed the bedroom door and slipped the lock in place, Aidan thought about Liam's increasing interest in sex over the past few days—since

Joey's arrival, in fact. What was up with that? Did Liam want Joey? Did Joey's presence incite something in Liam?

Returning to the bed, he climbed on and leaned over to kiss Liam. His partner's lips were dry, and Aidan licked his tongue along them to moisten them. He heard Liam groan beneath him.

As they kissed, Liam put his hand around the back of Aidan's head and pulled it close. They kissed, their tongues dueling, and Aidan felt his erection rise. He straddled Liam and began kissing his partner's chin, then nuzzling and licking his way down Liam's throat.

"You make me crazy, you know that?" Liam said.

"But in a good way," Aidan said.

"A very good way."

Aidan thought about Joey again, out in the living room. Was Liam hoping to draw Joey into their bedroom? Aidan hoped not. Joey was funny and cute and sexy—but Liam was all his, and he wasn't interested in sharing.

Aidan took Liam's left nipple in his mouth, grasping the gold ring with his teeth and tugging it, then licking around the nipple. Liam groaned. Yeah, see if Joey would do that to you, Aidan thought. He had to admit, though, that thinking of the hunky SEAL just on the other side of the bedroom door made his dick a little harder too.

Aidan reached down to Liam's crotch, where his stiff dick was still trapped in his shorts and jockstrap. Aidan massaged it with the palm of his hand. Liam arched his body up in response.

With Liam's right nipple in his mouth, Aidan reached down to undo Liam's shorts. Liam helped, raising his butt off the bed and pulling down the shorts and strap. Aidan lowered his dick to his partner's, rubbing the two of them together. Both were already horny, and their dicks were dripping precum.

Sweat began to drip down Aidan's chest, and he rubbed his hairy chest against Liam's smooth one. They kissed again, their bodies moving together. Liam pushed Aidan away, and said, "Turn around so I can suck you."

Aidan obliged, positioning his mouth at Liam's crotch and his dick at Liam's mouth. Liam licked Aidan's dick from the root to the tip, and the sensation was almost enough to push Aidan over the edge. They gobbled each other, and Aidan bobbed his head over Liam's dick as he pistoned his own dick into Liam's mouth.

He put his weight on his forearms, feeling the stretch and flex in his leg muscles. Up and down, up and down. The endorphins flooded his system at the connection with Liam, this man that he loved. His pulse raced as the force of the orgasm built in his guts.

Tiny cries escaped out of his mouth as he sucked Liam and the orgasm rose in his body. He came with a massive surge just as Liam shot off in his mouth. He licked Liam's dick once more, then pulled off, panting with exertion and the limited air flow. Liam pulled off his dick as well, and Aidan turned around and snuggled next to him. "We should get up," he said.

"Yeah," Aidan said. "We should. In a minute."

But they both dozed off and didn't wake for another hour. Then they showered and dressed, and by the time they went out to the living room to join Joey and Maks, it was early afternoon. The two of them were sitting at the kitchen table eating pizza.

"We saved you a couple of slices," Joey said. "Though if you'd slept any later. we'd have had to call room service again."

"How are you, Maks?" Aidan asked, taking a seat at the table next to the teenager. "Feeling better?"

"I am still feeling a little sick, and I am scared if those men will come for me again. Am I going back to school?"

"I hope so," Aidan said. "We're just waiting to hear from your father."

Liam picked up his cell and checked the display. "Shit. While we were in the shower, we missed two calls from Ullyanov. Your father is probably flipping out, Maks."

"Maybe it means that the recommendation is signed and sealed, and we can take Maks back to school," Aidan said.

"Ever the optimist." Liam ate a slice of pizza as he pressed the speed dial for Bazarov's assistant. He pressed the speaker button so everyone could hear the call.

"Where are you?" Ullyanov demanded, without even saying hello. "I have been calling you."

"We've got Maks in a safe location," Liam said. "Has his father signed the recommendation yet?"

"Where exactly are you?"

Liam looked at Aidan, who frowned. Why was Ullyanov so insistent?

"Like I said, we're safe," Liam said. "Is there still a threat?"

"You should take Maks back to the school," Ullyanov said. "Everything is fine. His father will call him later."

"Is my father there?" Maks asked.

"He is a very busy man, Maksat," Ullyanov said. "He will call you."

He disconnected, leaving the four of them looking at each other.

"That was strange," Aidan said.

Liam finished the last slice of pizza. "But he gave us our orders. Let's pack up and get back to Bizerte."

"You guys sure don't stay in one place for long," Joey said. He stood up. "Come on, Maks, let's start loading the car."

Aidan thought it was funny how Maks followed the big SEAL along like a little puppy. Maybe kidnapping had been a good thing for him. He was certainly a lot friendlier and more cooperative.

It took them an hour to get the SUV packed up and check out of the hotel. "You are sure it will be safe for me at the school?" Maks asked as they circled around the airport to get back to the Cairo-Dakar Highway.

"We'll still be there to look after you," Aidan said.

Maks turned to Joey. "And you too?"

"I have to get back to work soon, sport," Joey said, ruffling the teen's hair. "But these guys will take good care of you."

Maks leaned in toward Joey, and Aidan could just hear him say, "But they are, you know, homosexuals. You are not."

Joey laughed. "Homosexual or not, Liam can beat the shit out of anybody who comes after you. And Aidan's smarter than me and Liam put together."

Maks flushed crimson and leaned back against the door, his head down. Aidan couldn't help feeling a little pissed. They had saved Maks from the kidnappers, and all he cared about was what he and Liam did behind closed doors.

Had they been a little too loud that morning? Had Maks only figured out they were gay because they shared a bed at the hotel? Or had he known back at school? Aidan tried to remember the week at the monastery, but the events of the last few days had crowded out his memories. Liam had kept Maks from being picked up by the white van in Bizerte. The girls had clustered around Liam in his vest, awed by his muscular chest.

The other faculty had known—he remembered Monica's surprise when the subject came up at dinner on Friday. Did it matter what anybody thought? They'd been hired to do a job, and they'd done it. Who cared if they were gay or not?

Liam turned onto the highway in the neighborhood called Ariana, and from there they had miles of empty highway up to Bizerte. Aidan sat back against the front seat, Joey and Maks quiet in the back, Liam focused on driving.

Just after they passed the small town of Al-Aliyah, more than halfway to Bizerte, Aidan turned around to say something to Joey and spotted a white van closing in on them from behind. "Liam," he said. "White van behind us. You think it could be the same one?"

Maks turned to look out the rear window. "They are still coming for me? Will they take me again?"

"It's okay, sport," Joey said. "Nobody's taking you away while we're here."

"Everybody hold on," Liam said. "Here's a little physics lesson for you, Maks. If you're driving fast enough, turning the wheel won't stop a car from continuing forward. If you go too fast and turn too hard, the tires lose their connection to the pavement, causing the car to skid."

Aidan braced himself against the side door, knowing what was coming. "We call this move a J-turn," Liam said. "I'm going to spin the car 180 degrees, so we're facing back the way we were going."

"Hoo-ah," Joey said. "You're going to love this, Maks."

Liam slowed a little, letting the van catch up, then quickly turned the wheel, slewing the SUV around onto the median, then back onto the highway, facing back toward Tunis.

Aidan felt the g-forces pushing him in all directions, and thought for a minute he might throw up. But then the turn was over and Liam hit the accelerator.

"Don't try this back in Ashgabat," Liam said to Maks. Aidan turned and looked at Maks, who was looking pale, then through the back window. The van imitated their moves.

"Fasten your seat belts," Liam said. "It's going to be a bumpy ride."

"Jesus Christ," Joey said. "Bette Davis?"

"Bette Davis can't drive like I can," Liam said.

Offensive Driving

Liam was irritated more than anything else. It was like playing the Whac-A-Mole arcade game he'd loved as a kid. Murat Dvorkin kept popping up no matter how many times he got swatted down. Hadn't he gotten the message from whomever hired him that the recommendation had been put in, that Maks was in the clear?

What we have here, he thought, is a failure to communicate. What movie was that from? He pushed that thought away and focused on driving. He'd been one of the best drivers on the SEAL squad, and he had a sturdy SUV and a powerful engine at his disposal. Dvorkin, if that's who it was behind him, was in a rusty old van. If Liam couldn't ditch him, he deserved to have his license taken away.

He remembered the accident he'd seen on the way to Bizerte the first time. How could he use the road's strengths and weaknesses to his advantage? The divided highway ran through miles of sparse scrubland, with visibility far ahead and behind. There was an intermittent flow of traffic, mostly commercial vehicles ranging from small vans to semitrailers.

An 18-wheeler zoomed past on its way north, the air current rocking the SUV. Liam tried to visualize the road ahead. There was an interchange with the P8—a smaller road that ran roughly parallel to the Cairo-Dakar Highway. Was he better off on the local road?

He glanced in his rearview mirror. He saw Joey leaning toward Maks, speaking to him in low tones. Through the back window, he saw the white van.

"How did they know we'd be on this road?" Aidan asked.

"Ullyanov is the only person who knew we'd be on our way to Bizerte," Liam said. "He didn't know where we were, but chances were we went to ground somewhere in Tunis, and this is the only road north."

"I never like that man," Maks said. "He come work for my father last year as assistant, and quickly he is almost like my father's—how you say—left hand?"

"Right hand," Aidan said. He leaned over to Liam. "Last time they came at us from two directions. You think that's what they're going to try today?"

"I don't know. They thought we'd be going toward the monastery, but by turning around, we've avoided any trap they have set up there. But I still have to ditch the van before we get close to Tunis."

"Any ideas?" Aidan asked.

"There's a cloverleaf up ahead, where the highway meets the P8. I'm going to try something there."

"There's a Jersey term for you," Aidan said. "Cloverleaf."

"You know what they say. You can take the boy out of Jersey, but you can't take the Jersey out of the boy."

"Channel that thought." Aidan pulled the map from the glove compartment and traced his finger over their route. When he looked up, they were approaching the cloverleaf.

"This could get ugly," Liam said. "But Maks, I want you to believe that I know what I'm doing, all right?"

"I believe you," Maks said in a small voice.

"I'm going to use this cloverleaf to turn around so that I'm behind the van, and then I'm going to clip him on the rear bumper or his fender right near the taillight. I don't want to initiate a full-blown crash, because I don't want to put our own car out of commission."

"This is going to be cool, Maks," Joey said. "Way better than a video game."

Liam glanced in the rearview mirror. Maks didn't look like he was buying Joey's line. The white van was coming up fast behind them.

"What we're aiming for is what the cops call the PIT maneuver, for precision immobilization technique," Liam said. "We're going to knock the van's rear end off balance and send him fishtailing off the road, ideally facing the wrong direction."

"You have done this before?" Maks asked.

Joey reached into the cargo area of the SUV and started piling bags around him and Maks. "Liam's the best at this. But we might need a little extra padding.

And this will keep the stuff in the back from flying around and hitting us."

Liam saw Aidan brace himself against the door again as they took the turn into the cloverleaf, going a lot faster than the posted speed. The old van couldn't take the turn so fast, and it slowed down. Liam sped up and made a full circle, coming up behind the van as it was just coming out of the cloverleaf.

"Brace for impact." Liam slammed the accelerator pedal down and turned the wheel so that the SUV's right front bumper slammed into the left rear fender of the white van. The SUV shook with the impact, and he struggled to maintain control, swinging the SUV away as the van shot off the roadway. He got a quick glimpse of the man he knew as Dvorkin gripping the van's steering wheel.

The van spun around 180 degrees, continuing its trajectory off the road and into the scrub. Liam slowed just enough to maintain control of the SUV and got back on the highway toward Tunis. In the rearview mirror, he saw the white van finally come to a stop. With luck, Dvorkin had damaged an axle.

Joey began clapping slowly, and Aidan, then Maks joined in. "Good job, sweetheart," Aidan said, leaning over to kiss him on the cheek. "Now I say we head back to the Golden Sands. Nobody knows we're there, and it's pretty secure as hotels go."

"Make it so," Liam said.

Aidan laughed and retrieved his cell phone from the SUV's floor. He called the hotel and made a new reservation for the same villa. "Sorry, our plans changed at the last minute," Liam heard him say. "Yes, we're going to stay for a while now. Leave our departure date open."

It took another half hour to get back to the Golden Sands, Liam constantly checking his rearview mirror to make sure that the white van had not returned, that there was no other suspicious vehicle following them. He didn't pull up to the hotel's security gate until he was sure they had not been tailed.

Joey took Maks inside the villa, promising him a rematch on the video game. Once again Liam and Aidan unloaded their gear from the SUV. Joey had cleaned up the backseat as best he could, but one of the bags had come open and there were bullets and flashlights and other gear scattered under the front seats. "This is getting old," Liam said as they tossed everything back in the bag.

"I hear you," Aidan said. "What are we going to do now?"

"I don't know. I don't know who we can trust. What if Ullyanov's working for the bad guys?"

"We could have Maks try his father," Aidan said. "He's paying us, after all. He has no reason to hurt his own son. Or at least he has no reason to hire us to keep his son safe if he's the one trying to get him killed."

"Makes sense to me." He grabbed a couple of duffels and started for the door. Aidan picked up the rest and followed him in.

They dumped all the gear in the living room, where Joey and Maks sat on the sofa, waiting for the video game to start. "Maks, we want you to call your father," Aidan said. "You have his number in your phone, don't you?"

"He will want me to go back to Ashgabat."

"You don't know that," Liam said.

Maks crossed his arms over his chest. "I know my father. I have to fight much just to go to the institute."

The TV lit up with the introductory screen for the same video game Joey and Maks had been playing that morning, which Liam saw was called *Red Dead Redemption*. He hadn't played a video game in years, and he envied Joey the casual freedom to hang out with the client while he and Aidan handled the heavy lifting.

But that was what they got paid for, Liam thought as Maks picked up his controller.

Aidan used the remote to shut the TV off. "Maks. Make the call."

Maks pulled his cell phone from his pocket. "No signal," he said and put it back.

Aidan said nothing, but Liam could see him glaring at the teen like a misbehaving schoolboy. Maks's shoulders sagged as he turned away from Aidan's look.

He took the phone out again and hit a couple of buttons. They all heard the ringing, and then the sound of his father's voice mail picking up.

Maks said something in Turkmen. As he was finishing, his voice rose a little and despite the unfamiliar language Aidan could hear the emotion. "I leave him message," Maks said when he finished the call. "That I am okay, and please to call me."

"Thank you," Aidan said and switched the TV back on. He and Liam began sorting through the bags as Joey and Maks pounded their game controllers and talked trash to each other.

It was dinnertime by then, so Aidan called room service and ordered hamburgers and sodas for them. Liam felt he could really use a couple of beers, but not with unknown threats to the client still out there.

He was unloading a bag in the master bedroom when Aidan came in. "Do we have a picture of Ullyanov?" Aidan asked.

"I don't think so. Why?"

"I'm thinking Richard could use that image recognition software on a picture of Ullyanov, see if that's his real name and if there's anything out there about him."

"Good idea. Didn't you find a Web site for Bazarov's businesses? There could be a picture of Ullyanov there."

Aidan sat on the bed with the computer on his lap. There was wireless high-speed Internet access throughout the hotel property, so he was able to connect easily. When Liam finished unpacking, he sat on the bed next to Aidan. "I couldn't find a picture on the company site, but I did get his full name. Vadim Ullyanov. Then I searched for pictures of anybody by that name. Recognize any of them?"

Liam watched as Aidan scrolled through the photos. Each man was too old, too young, too dark or too fair to match the man he had met at the Tunis airport. Then he saw a man in a group shot who looked familiar. "There. That one." He pointed at the screen.

Aidan clicked on the thumbnail, and the page containing the picture came up. All in Cyrillic. "Shit," Liam said.

"Hold on," Aidan said. "It's still loading." A tool bar appeared at the top of the screen offering to translate the page into English. He clicked the translate button.

It was Ullyanov, all right, though a few years younger. The photo, dated July 11, 2005, showed a group of men at the ground-breaking for an industrial plant in Chechnya. The oldest man in the picture, the one who was clearly the boss, was named Ruslan Popov. "Why does that name sound familiar?" Liam asked.

"Hold on." Aidan opened Word on the laptop and pulled up the notes he had been keeping on the project. "Here it is," he said. "Ruslan Popov. He owns Stroika Popov, and he wants Nuryagdy Bazarov to recommend him for the pipeline construction."

"The little bastard," Liam said. "Ullyanov has been working for Popov all along."

Unexpected Guest

"Should we show Maks this picture?" Aidan asked.

"Absolutely."

Aidan carried the laptop, and they went out to the living room just as the villa's doorbell rang. Liam held up his hand, and everyone stopped where they were. He crossed to the front door and checked through the peephole. "Dinner," he said.

The delivery boy pushed a cart into the room, setting everything up on the dining room table. Liam thought it was funny to see such a fancy presentation—china plates, crystal glasses, heavy silverware—for a dinner of burgers, fries, and sodas, but he didn't say anything.

Aidan waited until they were finished eating to ask Maks, "Do you know anything about Vadim Ullyanov?"

Maks looked up. "I do not even know his first name. He is always just called Ullyanov."

"But he's Russian? Not Turkmen?"

"Yes, he is Russian. I think maybe he go to school in Ashgabat for some time. He speaks good Turkmen, though sometimes he make mistakes."

Aidan opened the computer and pulled up the picture. "This is Ullyanov, isn't it?"

Maks looked at the screen. "Yes. Who are these other men?"

"That's Ruslan Popov," Liam said, pointing. "The man who wants your father's recommendation."

Maks looked from Liam to Aidan to Joey. "I do not understand."

"The government in Turkmenistan is going to build a gas pipeline under the Caspian Sea, to connect to one in Chechnya," Liam said. "Two companies want the contract to build this pipeline. One company is Russian, the other Chinese."

Maks nodded. "Yes, my father tells me this."

"Your father was supposed to recommend one of the two companies to the government today. He favored the Chinese company."

"Not the one this man owns, Popov?"

"No."

Liam could see Maks thinking. He was a pretty smart kid, it seemed. "So Russian company try to make me kidnapped to pressure my father?"

Liam and Aidan both nodded.

"And Ullyanov, he work once for this Russian company?"

"That's the way it looks," Liam said.

"My father do not know this?"

"We don't know," Aidan said. "But it doesn't make sense that he would hire us to protect you if he did."

Maks pulled his cell phone out of his pocket once more and punched buttons. The phone rang once, then went to voice mail. Liam couldn't translate the words the boy used, but he could understand the emotion, the way Maks said the name Ullyanov with such venom. Gone was the near weepiness of the first message Maks had left. Liam smiled as Maks closed the phone.

"What do we do now?" Joey asked.

"We wait," Liam said.

They all watched a movie. As it was ending, Maks's phone rang. "Is my father." He answered in Turkmen, speaking eagerly to his father. Liam watched his face closely as Maks listened. The boy's mouth turned down at the corners.

"He is already knowing about Ullyanov," Maks said.

He listened more, then said, "He is here in Tunis, at airport. He wants to come here to me."

Liam looked at Aidan. Bazarov was the client, after all. Aidan found a piece of hotel stationery and handed it to Maks, who read the hotel's name and address to his father. "He is getting car and driver to come here," he said when he had ended the call.

"How long will it take him to get here?" Aidan asked.

"Half an hour or so," Liam said.

"We ought to get this place cleaned up then. Maks, you and Joey make sure your room is shipshape. I'll take the kitchen and living room; Liam, you handle the bedroom."

"What is mean shipshape?" Maks asked.

Joey laughed. "It means Aidan's getting bossy, sport." He stood up. "Come on; we've got our marching orders."

Just about a half hour later, the security guard at the gate called to announce Bazarov was there. "Yes, send him in," Liam said.

Liam walked to the front door and waited. A black Lincoln Town Car appeared along the winding drive, and Maks came to stand just behind him. When the car pulled up, Bazarov jumped out and Maks squirmed under Liam's arm to rush to his father.

It was a touching scene, but Liam wanted both father and son safely under cover as quickly as possible. He paid off the limo driver as Aidan ushered Bazarov and Maks into the villa.

As Liam had suspected, Bazarov spoke better English than he had let on at the airport. They all sat in the living room to hear his story.

"This morning I hear Ullyanov tell you to take Maks back to the school. I think this is wrong, because I have not signed letter yet making recommendation. I ask Ullyanov this."

He pointed to a bruise on his right cheek. "He hit me," he said. "Then he run away. I know I must come to Tunisia immediately to make sure Maks is all right."

Aidan showed Bazarov the laptop, with the picture of Ullyanov and Popov.

"He is rat bastard!" Bazarov said. "All this time he is working for Popov. I know I am right not to trust Russians."

"Did you sign the recommendation?" Aidan asked.

"No. I leave Ashgabat too fast."

"So there is still a chance that Popov's man will go after Maks again," Liam said.

Bazarov put his arm around his son. "You must protect him. There is no way I will do business with Popov."

"I think we're safe here for tonight," Liam said. "No one followed us here. But tomorrow you should make your recommendation to the Turkmen government, and maybe that will call Popov off."

"I will make call in the morning."

It was almost eleven by then, and Maks yawned. "I'll bunk down out here," Joey said, standing up. "You can have my bed, Mr. Bazarov."

"I can get room in hotel," Bazarov said.

"I'd rather we all stayed together, at least for tonight," Liam said. "Safety in numbers."

Bazarov and Maks went into the bedroom. "I'm worried," Aidan said. "Dvorkin is a sharp operator. Do you think there's a chance he knows where we are?"

"How could he?" Joey asked. "Nobody followed us after Liam ran the van off the road."

Aidan and Liam looked at each other. "Bazarov."

"You think he's going to put his son in danger?" Joey asked.

Liam shook his head. "No, but if Ullyanov figured out that Bazarov was coming to Tunis, he could have tipped off Dvorkin. He or one of his men could have followed Bazarov from the airport."

"Should we get out of here?" Aidan asked.

Liam looked to Joey. Both of them had been through the same kind of training. "This place is the best defense we've got, for now," Joey said. "Guards at the gate. We'll keep a good watch."

"Joey's right. If we try and get out of here tonight, we could be driving into a trap. And we don't have any place any better set up." He shook his head. "I hate the way Dvorkin is always putting us on the defensive."

Joey volunteered to take the first watch. "Be careful," Liam said. "This guy has a million tricks up his sleeve." He told Joey about the first kidnap attempt in the souk. "Then he threw a Molotov cocktail in the back courtyard at the monastery, trying to flush us out."

"He's still no match for the both of us," Joey said.

"From your mouth to God's ears," Aidan said.

"Don't forget Allah," Liam said. "We're in a Muslim country. And we can use all the divine help we can get."

Firefight

Liam, Aidan, and Joey walked around the villa, evaluating the threats and possibilities. "How would you approach this if you were Dvorkin?" Aidan asked.

Liam looked out at the Mediterranean and remembered again the operation he and Joey had carried out in Bizerte years before. "I'd come in from the ocean. You avoid the guards at the gate that way. Powerboat, so that I could leave fast once I had Maks."

"But you'd have to turn the engines off for the incoming," Joey said. "You'd need a dinghy to row in, and another guy to wait with the boat for your signal, to come in and pick you up."

"Can Dvorkin get a boat at this time of night?" Aidan asked.

Liam laughed. "This guy can do anything."

"How do we protect ourselves?"

"If we had the time—and the gear—we'd rig up some kind of motion detector at the beach. But we can't get anything like that in place tonight. All we can do is be prepared."

Back in the living room, they surveyed their weapons. Aidan and Liam both had pistols with extra rounds of ammunition. Liam had also picked up another they kept at the house for Joey to use. "If there's a firefight, your job is to keep the clients safe," Liam said to Aidan.

"Where do you want me?"

"Clients in the guest bath," Joey said. "No windows there. If Aidan stays outside the door, he can see the front door, and in the other direction he can see through the master bedroom."

"Works for me," Aidan said, and Liam nodded. "Where are you guys going to be?"

"Wherever we need to be," Liam said. "If they come from the sea, we can use the furniture on the patio for cover."

"They could come in by land too," Aidan said. "Even I could get past the guard at the front gate."

"He's got a point," Joey said. "Whoever is on patrol has to keep an eye on both approaches."

They decided on three-hour shifts. Liam and Aidan went into the bedroom around midnight, both of them lying on the bed fully clothed and ready to jump into action if necessary. With his years of experience in the unpredictable world of the SEALs, Liam had trained himself to fall asleep almost on command, and he was out cold within minutes after hitting the bed.

Joey woke him at three for his shift. Liam rolled out of bed, careful not to wake Aidan, and followed his friend out to the living room. "Anything happening?"

"It's been quiet," Joey said. "I'm going to bunk down on the sofa. You hear anything, you wake me ASAP."

"Will do."

Liam walked out the front door. The hotel grounds were almost spookily quiet, just the sound of the surf rolling in. He circled the house once, checking, then walked to the water's edge. The tide chart the hotel had provided said high tide would be at four. There were gentle waves rolling in—not enough to surf, but enough to make trouble for a small boat trying to reach shore.

He stood there, regulating his breathing and taking in everything about the area around him, identifying the smell of the salt water and the pieces of wet seaweed that had washed up on the shore. There was a faint undertone of coconut tanning lotion, and motor oil that had stained the parking yard.

A sand rat scampered across the beach just ahead of him. A small black and gray lizard with bulging eyes raced out of the undergrowth, a bat in hot pursuit. The lizard slipped beneath a spiny aloe, and the bat swooped upward and away.

Liam was enjoying the sense of oneness with his environment when he heard an unfamiliar sound, the low rumble of a diesel engine. He strained to locate it. Was it a piece of maintenance equipment from the hotel? A car out on the drive that circled around the property? Or a boat out on the water?

The sound stopped abruptly. Liam strained, but he could not hear it anymore. But he did hear the telltale sound of waves lapping against a boat's hull, and then oars dipping into the water.

This was it. They were on their way.

He ran back to the front of the house, rousing Joey from the sofa as he went to the bedroom. He woke

Aidan, grabbed his pistol and his night vision goggles, and exited through the sliding glass doors. Aidan locked them behind him.

Joey was next to him a moment later, his gun in his hand and his night vision goggles around his neck. Neither of them spoke, both straining to hear the sound of the approaching boat. Instead they heard Aidan inside, waking Bazarov and Maks and herding them to the guest bathroom.

"Shit," Liam said under his breath.

"You hear it?"

"The boat?" Liam asked, but even as he did, he heard the sound of a car door opening.

"Motherfuckers," Joey said. "They're coming at us from both directions."

"One if by land and two if by sea," Liam said. "You take the front of the house; I'll stay here."

Joey turned and moved away, and Liam strained once more to hear the sound of the boat. Dvorkin was smart; he was using the motion of the incoming tide to bring the boat, only using the oars to steer, so there was little to hear.

Liam raised the night vision goggles and surveyed the ocean. Coming toward him, he saw an inflatable dinghy with two men inside, one at each oar. He wished he'd brought a rifle with him, but most personal protection was done at close quarters, and the only rifle he owned was locked up in a secret compartment above the bedroom of the house in Tunis.

He was most comfortable shooting the pistol at no more than fifty yards. He planned to aim for the men, with the fallback of puncturing the inflatable raft and dumping Dvorkin—if that's who was in the raft—and his accomplice in the surf.

The raft moved slowly toward the shore, riding the crests of the incoming surf. Liam forced himself to remain still behind his cover of palm and aloe, his gaze trained on the men at the oars. At least there were only two. But he could not see their faces at that distance, so he didn't know if the two were Dvorkin and Oman or merely decoys, with Dvorkin planning his main approach by land.

He hated not knowing how things were going at the front of the house. How many men were coming at them? How were they armed? If he were Dvorkin, where would he be at this point? In the boat or in a car?

What was Aidan doing in the house? Had he locked Bazarov and Maks in the bathroom? He had no idea there were two teams on their way, so he might attempt to help Liam out against the waterborne intruders, leaving the clients vulnerable to attack from the front.

In the SEALs, one of the most important lessons he had learned was to trust the men around him, not second-guess them or worry about their skills. Joey was not the best shot from their team, nor the strongest in hand-to-hand combat. But he was the most dedicated, determined soldier Liam knew. Liam knew he could trust Joey with anything—including his own life.

Aidan wasn't a trained solder like he and Joey were, but Aidan had a strength of character and an inventiveness that had seen him through a number of tough situations. At this point, he had to hope that he had trained Aidan well enough.

Liam looked back at the raft. It was almost within range, though he still couldn't make out the faces of either man. He was left guessing—did either man's silhouette match Dvorkin's? What kind of weapons would they have with them in the boat?

The night was still eerily quiet, even though Liam knew there was movement going on around him. The lizards and bats had disappeared, perhaps sensing the oncoming trouble.

Then he heard gunfire erupt around the front, recognizing the distinctive sound of the .357 Sig as Joey shot. Almost reflexively Liam aimed at the men in the raft and began shooting, emptying the ten bullets in the magazine.

He winged one of the men in the upper arm and watched him fall backward. The other man raised a rifle to his shoulder and began spraying the beach randomly, unable to make out Liam's position.

Liam slid the empty magazine out of the gun and dropped it in his pocket, replacing it with a full one. From the front yard, he heard answering fire to Joey's Sig. An approaching light caught the corner of his eye, and he dropped the goggles to look toward it.

It was the headlight of a golf cart, coming at them from the direction of the main hotel building. The gunfire must have attracted security.

He turned back to the water. The boat was only about twenty yards away, and the man with the rifle jumped out, holding the weapon above his head and wading through the surf. Liam aimed at body mass and shot, but nothing stopped the man. He must be wearing armor, Liam thought.

The golf cart stopped a few hundred yards up the drive, the guard smart enough not to get into a firefight. Liam heard him on the radio, speaking excitedly in Arabic. Good. That meant there would be reinforcements at some point. He just had to hold off the man with the rifle until then.

The second magazine was empty, and he replaced it with a third. He slipped the goggles back on and aimed at the man's head. He didn't like that kind of shot; it was too risky and too deadly. On a moral level, he didn't want to kill anyone unless he absolutely had to. But with body armor, there wasn't much choice. He took aim.

"Front is clear!" Joey called.

Liam squeezed the trigger in quick succession. His first three shots went wide of the target, but the fourth hit the man square in the center of the forehead. He collapsed at the edge of the surf.

Liam scanned the surf for the inflatable raft. It was sinking fast, a few hundred yards off shore, the wounded man bailing frantically in a losing battle. Farther out, the powerboat that had delivered them gunned the engine and tore off.

"Still one bogey in the water," Liam called. He had no interest in dragging the man in the surf forward to the sand. He kept his eyes on the man in the water, who alternated paddling with bailing, making little progress with either job.

He took his cell from his pocket. From the glowing display, he saw it was not quite four a.m. He dialed Faisal Qasim's number.

Faisal sounded groggy. "Yes?" he said in Arabic. "Who is this?"

Liam gave him a quick explanation, and Faisal groaned. "I suppose you want me to come out there."

"Would be nice."

"For you," Faisal said. "I will make some calls and be there in an hour."

Liam ended the call and walked slowly to the water's edge, his pistol still in his hand, to where the body of the man he had shot rested facedown in the incoming tide. He leaned down and felt for a pulse at the man's neck. There was none.

If he'd still been a SEAL, he and Joey would have stripped the man of his weapons and disappeared into the night. But instead he left the man where he was, his rifle fallen by his side, and raised the goggles to his face, looking out to the man in the boat.

At last he could get a clear view of the man's face. It was Mushtaq Oman, the man who had been keeping Maks prisoner in the slaughterhouse.

"Come on in, pal," Liam said to the night. "We've got some unfinished business."

Police Investigation

When the shooting began, Aidan had felt a surge of adrenaline. He was standing guard in front of the bathroom door, as he'd been told, his pistol in his right hand. It seemed like there were shots fired at the front and back of the house. That didn't make sense, though; Liam had told them to expect a water landing.

Where was Liam? Where was Joey? Who was shooting? So much uncertainty made Aidan jittery, and once again he reconsidered the whole bodyguard thing in favor of teaching as he stood there. He'd been a little jealous that as soon as Joey showed up, he'd become Liam's second in command. Sometimes it was as if Aidan didn't exist except as an errand boy.

In his head, he knew Joey was a soldier like Liam, with years of training and military experience. Joey and Liam shared a shorthand based on the missions they'd done together. Aidan had a two-week bodyguard course under his belt, plus a little over a year of on-the-job training with Liam. There was no comparison.

But there was still something about Liam's easy connection with Joey that made Aidan uncomfortable. He was pretty sure that Joey was, as he had said, one hundred percent straight, and there was no danger that Liam would abandon Aidan for his SEAL buddy. But down deep in his heart, he couldn't help but be nervous.

He stood in front of the bathroom door, not knowing what was going on. They only had two walkie-talkies, and Liam and Joey had those. All Aidan could do was strain for the sounds of gunfire and wait.

The front door slammed open, and Aidan raised his gun, his heart rate soaring.

"Got any rope?" Joey asked, sticking his head inside. "I've got two guys out here I need to tie up."

"Is Liam all right?"

"He's watching out the back for somebody in the surf." Joey stepped in the living room and looked around.

"Right. We don't have rope, but we can rip up sheets." Aidan opened the bathroom door. "It's clear. Maks, can you help Joey? Pull the sheets off your bed and take them out to him."

Maks nodded, and his father said, "I will help. Come, Maksat."

Joey retreated back outside to watch his prisoners, and Aidan opened the sliding glass doors to check on Liam. Fortunately his partner looked intact, standing there with the night vision goggles on his face, looking out at the water.

Without benefit of the goggles, all Aidan could see was a man in a rubber boat that looked like it was sinking. Then he noticed the body of a man at the water's edge. Somehow, without going near him, Aidan knew the man was dead.

He wanted to hug Liam, just to make sure he was all there, but he knew Liam wouldn't want the distraction. "As soon as I heard the gunfire, I called the hotel front desk and asked them to call the cops. I told them they'd better send an ambulance too."

"Good idea."

"Joey's got two guys out front he needs to tie up," Aidan said. "Maks and his father are tearing up sheets for Joey to use." He waited a second. "What happened?"

"Dvorkin thought he could get us with a two-pronged attack. He failed."

Aidan looked from the water to the dead man, then back to Liam. "You'll be all right back here?" Aidan said. It was more a statement than a question.

"Yup."

Aidan went back into the house. He had never killed anyone, and he couldn't imagine what was going through Liam's head. He'd surely killed men while he was a SEAL; did another matter? From the bigger man's stance and the gruffness in his voice, Aidan had a feeling it did.

Out front there were two men lying on the ground, both bleeding. Aidan didn't recognize either one but assumed they were among the men who had kidnapped Maks. Joey was using some of the torn linen to stanch a wound in one man's abdomen while Maks and his father were tying the other's arms and legs and positioning him against the base of a palm tree.

Joey had shot one in the abdomen, the other in both arms and the upper chest. They looked almost like mummies, the way Maks and Bazarov had wrapped them up so carefully with torn strips of bedsheets.

A police car approached with flashing lights. By then both wounded men had been tied up. Joey and Aidan had holstered their guns and were waiting with Maks and Bazarov as the police car pulled up next to their rented SUV, followed by a hotel security guard in a golf cart.

Joey's Arabic was almost as good as Liam's, so he took on the responsibility of telling the cops what had happened. Aidan didn't understand it all, but he could tell Joey was being very careful.

"There is one more man from our team out back," Joey said. "Watching two more attackers."

The security guard gaped openmouthed at the destruction around him. One officer went back to his car and radioed for more assistance, then went around the back of the villa. Joey called, "Police on the way, Billy," and the remaining cop launched into a stream of Arabic invective.

"Just protecting your man," Joey said calmly.

The two cops were overwhelmed with the multiple victims and their confusion over what had gone on, and they did little more than make sure everyone stayed in place until two more cars arrived.

An older cop took control, asking Liam, Joey, and Aidan to surrender their weapons and placing the five of them in the villa's living room, guarded by a police officer to be sure they did not speak. He dispatched one officer to guard the dead man, and two more to wait for Mushtaq Oman to come to shore.

An ambulance arrived to take the two men Joey had shot to the hospital. The older cop instructed the attendants that they were suspected of criminal activity, and sent one of the officers along with them to guard them until they could be interviewed.

Faisal drove up as the ambulance was leaving. He looked tired to Aidan, though the creases in his military shirt were crisp, his black shoes spit shined as always. "You will have an explanation for all this," he said to Liam in Arabic.

Liam bowed slightly. "Of course."

Faisal spoke rapidly to the hotel security guard, who stepped away and began speaking on his radio. The two officers who had been waiting at the shore appeared from around the corner of the villa, escorting Oman, who was drenched and shivering. He began speaking rapidly in Arabic too complicated for Aidan to understand. Faisal barked at him to be quiet, and he shut his mouth in midsentence and hung his head.

A second ambulance arrived, and the attendants were dispatched to the shore to pick up Dvorkin's body. "Get this man a towel," Faisal told one of the cops, who went into the villa. Aidan felt a small sense of violation, even as he recognized he had to keep quiet about it.

By the time the cop came back with a beach towel for Oman, the two ambulance attendants had returned with Dvorkin's body on a litter. In the shine of the police headlights, Liam leaned down and took a good look at the man's face. Then he stood up again. "His name is Murat Dvorkin, and he's an independent operative based in Ashgabat, Turkmenistan."

"This is the man you asked me about?" Faisal asked.

Liam nodded. "I believe he entered Tunisia with a fake passport under the name Nazar Rakhimov."

Faisal nodded at the two attendants, who loaded Dvorkin's body into the second ambulance. The hotel security guard returned and confirmed that the next-door villa was empty, and Faisal commandeered it.

Each of them was placed in a separate room, with a policeman as guard, until he finished all his interviews. Aidan was stuck in the guest bedroom of their villa amid the debris of discarded blankets and torn sheets. He paced around the room anxiously, worried about his own fate, Liam's and Joey's, avoiding any contact with the police officer guarding him, who sat at the desk and said nothing.

Even though Liam knew Faisal and trusted him, Aidan didn't. It wouldn't take much to arrest the whole bunch of them and throw them in jail until all the forensics and other investigations were complete. Aidan hadn't shot anyone himself, and his handgun was licensed. But who was to say the police would believe the whole story?

Liam had killed a man. He had a permit for his gun, and he had committed the act while defending himself and his client. Even so, homicide was a serious business.

Joey was a US Navy SEAL on active duty, even if he was on a temporary furlough. His involvement could lead to military discipline and perhaps an uncomfortable situation for the US government.

Bazarov and his son were citizens of Turkmenistan. Who knew what kind of relations their country had with Tunisia? Would they be able to walk away easily from the situation?

The bedroom door opened shortly after sunrise, and the officer at the desk stood up. "You will come here, please," the officer at the door said.

Faisal was sitting at the table surrounded by piles of paper as Aidan entered the kitchen. "You have had a busy evening," he said. "I will try to make this quick."

A tape recorder sat in the middle of the table, and as Aidan walked over, Faisal ejected one tape and put in a new one. "Sit down, please," Faisal said, motioning to the chair across from him. "You prefer we speak in English?"

"Yes, please."

The living room was flooded with sunlight, and in the distance, Aidan could hear the sound of children playing in the surf. It was almost surreal to him, to sit in such beautiful surroundings and be interviewed by the police about an attack and a man's death.

They went quickly through the basics. Aidan gave his name, his age, and his address for the tape, then explained how they had all come to be at the Golden Sands hotel. It took nearly an hour, with stops to find Madame Abboud's phone number, the address for the monastery, and so on.

Finally they came to the events of the night. "What I do not understand," Faisal said after Aidan had explained. "Is why you did not call the police last night when you were worried."

"We had no evidence and nothing to report," Aidan said. "We had no proof that Mr. Bazarov had been followed from the airport, and no evidence that Dvorkin had tracked us here otherwise."

"I had a man go out to the highway interchange near Dawwar al Huwayd," Faisal said. "There is evidence of an accident there, but nothing was reported by either party."

"What could we say?" Aidan said. "We already knew that the license plate for the van didn't match the registration. Did you look up the report from the kidnapping outside the monastery?"

"I am asking the questions, if you please," Faisal said. "Yes, I did. And I can tell you that a white van was found about a mile from the hotel with damage as Liam indicated to me. The license plates have been changed again, so they do not match the kidnapping incident, however."

He leaned back in his chair. "He is very good at what he does, your friend Liam."

"Yes. Without him, Maksat Bazarov might still be with his kidnappers. Or all of us might have been killed last night."

Faisal looked at him, then said, "Thank you for your cooperation. You may return to the bedroom now."

Aidan started to protest, but Faisal's black eyes glared at him and he gave in meekly. This time there was no one to guard him, but he still fretted over the others and what had happened to them.

Fathers and Sons

It was another two hours before a policeman opened the bedroom door again and brought Aidan back to the living room. Joey and Liam were there, and Maks and his father were coming out of the master bedroom. Faisal stood by the kitchen table.

"I will go back to Tunis and consider my report," he said. "Until then, you will all please stay here at this villa. I will leave a police officer outside."

All the police but one left, and Aidan called room service for breakfast for all of them. As they ate, Bazarov recounted his conversation with Faisal Qasim. "I explain that I hire you three to protect me and my son."

Aidan thought it was a nice gesture to include Joey in the mix—though probably Bazarov simply thought it was expedient to do so.

"I tell him about Ruslan Popov and the threats he make to me, to force me to recommend his company. This man seem very intelligent. I am sure he will make correct decision."

"Glad you feel that way," Liam said.

When they finished eating, Bazarov commandeered the laptop for his business purposes, setting himself up in the guest bedroom with his cell phone. Joey and Maks picked up their video game again, and Liam went into the master bedroom to exercise.

Aidan called Madame Abboud and told her what had happened. She didn't seem to care that armed men had shot at them or that they were still dealing with the police. "Your classes went untaught yesterday and today," she said. "You made an agreement to work for me, and you have put me in a very awkward position."

Aidan wanted to laugh but controlled himself. "I hope to be back tomorrow," he said. "If the police let us go."

"If there is a problem, you will let me know," Madame Abboud said and hung up. Aidan wondered if that meant she had some clout with the Tunisian police, or if she was just trying to figure out if she'd have to replace him.

He went into the master bedroom. Liam was on the floor doing one-handed push-ups. "Aren't you going to join me?" he asked. "You haven't been working out enough lately."

"I need to talk, not work out." Aidan sat down on the bed and waited for Liam to finish his set.

When he did, Liam sat up with his back against the wall. "What do you want to talk about?"

"Madame Abboud thinks I'm coming back to teach in Bizerte. Am I?"

"I don't know, Aidan. Are you?"

"What am I, Liam? Am I a teacher? A bodyguard?"

"Why can't you be both?" He stood up, then sat next to Aidan on the bed. "Do you think you can't do both those things? You've taught a couple of times for Madame Abboud already."

"It's not a question of whether I can do both. Can I do both well—or well enough?"

Liam nodded. "That's a good question. Only you can answer it, though."

"But what do you think? I know I'm not a great bodyguard. As soon as Joey showed up, you made him your partner. I just ran the errands."

"Is that how you feel?" Liam turned halfway on the bed to look at Aidan.

"My head says Joey is way more qualified to work with you than I am. But my heart says I want to be the one you come to for help."

Liam leaned across and kissed Aidan's cheek. "I come to you for way more than help planning an operation. Way more."

Aidan turned to face him. "You do? Really? Because most of the time, I don't feel like I'm pulling my weight."

"There's more to being a bodyguard than muscle or tactical skills, Aidan. You know that already. You have skills I don't have—the way your brain works, the compassion you have for people. We're not equals—we know that. But we complement each other. Together we're better than the sum of our parts." He took Aidan's hand. "And one of those parts is your ability to teach. It's a great talent, and I know it means a lot to you. We'll have to work together to make sure you can teach when you want to."

He smiled. "If you want to go back to Bizerte for the next five weeks, that's fine with me. We both signed contracts to work at the institute."

"But that was when Maks needed protection. Madame Abboud would probably release you if you want."

"We'll see how it works out. But I can see that this job means a lot to you, and I want you to be able to finish it."

"You're awfully good to me." Aidan leaned over and kissed Liam's lips. "In so many ways."

"You're not bad yourself," Liam said.

"Not bad!" Aidan pushed Liam backward on the bed. "Not bad!" He twisted around and straddled him.

"Aidan, the door," Liam said.

Aidan turned and saw it was wide open. He called, "Joey, do me a favor? Close the bedroom door for me?"

"I'm playing a game," Joey called. "If I put this controller down, Maks is going to cream me."

Aidan looked at Liam, and he could tell they both thought of cream in the same way. Resisting laughter, Liam bellowed, "Pause the goddamn game, Sheridan!"

"Fine." They heard Joey jump up from the sofa and stride across the room. "You better make this worth my while, Billy," he said as he slammed the door shut.

"Yeah," Aidan said. "Make this worth my while too." He leaned down and kissed Liam again. He didn't care that Joey was in the living room with Maks, that

Bazarov was in the next bedroom. All he cared about was having his partner in his arms.

Liam was sweaty from his exercise, and Aidan slid a hand down his partner's slick chest. Liam sighed beneath him. Aidan leaned back and pulled off his T-shirt, then shucked his shorts and his boxers. As he did, Liam lifted his ass from the bed and slid off his workout shorts and his jockstrap.

"Mmm," Aidan said, nestling down on top of Liam. "I could do this all day."

"Well, we are stuck here in this villa until Faisal lets us go."

Aidan kissed Liam again, then began sliding his body against his partner's. Liam was already hard, and his stiff, uncircumcised dick rubbed against Aidan's abdomen. Aidan pressed his dick against Liam's smooth thigh. They kissed passionately as they moved together, their sweat and precum lubricating them.

"You know I love you, whether you're a teacher or a bodyguard or a trash collector," Liam said into Aidan's neck.

"I love you so much," Aidan said. "I just want to be everything you want me to be."

"All I want you to be is you. The cute, goofy, smart, sexy guy I fell in love with."

Aidan's pulse quickened as he rubbed against Liam. He could tell from his partner's faster breathing that Liam was about to come, and that made him rub even harder against him.

They heard the volume of the video game increase out in the living room, and both of them looked at each other and laughed, then renewed their frottage. Aidan came first, biting down a whimpered cry and feeling his dick spurt against Liam's smooth skin. Then Liam came a moment later, panting and throwing his head back against the pillow.

"Big mess," Liam said as Aidan rolled off him and nestled next to him. He rubbed the pool of cum against his stomach. "What is the maid going to think of us?"

Aidan laughed. "Let's hope she's glad we're all alive. I know I am."

He rested his head against Liam's shoulder, and they dozed for an hour, waking to find themselves hot and sticky, with dried cum pooling in their pubic hair. They took a shower together and dressed, coming out to the living room just as room service delivered another pizza and the housekeeper arrived to clean the villa.

Bazarov joined them from the guest room, and they all ate with gusto. When they finished eating, they sat in the living room while the maid finished cleaning the kitchen area. She left shortly before five o'clock, and Aidan could tell Liam and Joey were getting antsy. Maks seemed happy to be able to spend time with his father, but Bazarov kept getting phone calls and trying to do business.

"I have much to do back in Ashgabat," Bazarov said when he finished another call. "I would like to return there tonight if this policeman will be finished with us. Perhaps I should speak with the Turkmen Embassy in Tunis."

"Faisal is a good man," Liam said. "I'm sure he's working on things."

"Will I be able to go back to the school when we are finished here?" Maks asked his father. Aidan had the feeling he was using English so that everyone could understand and so that he could use Aidan and Liam for leverage if he needed. He smiled to realize the son was probably almost as crafty as the father.

"You wish to?" Bazarov said.

"Yes, please."

Bazarov looked at Liam and Aidan. "You will go with him?"

"You hired us for six weeks," Liam said. "If you still want us, we'll go."

Bazarov nodded. "Even with this man Dvorkin stopped, I am still worried. Maks is my son, and I must protect him."

"We'll take care of him," Aidan said.

Faisal returned to the villa about a half hour later. "I am able to return your weapons to you, but I have just a few more questions for Liam and Aidan," he said. "The rest of you will please wait in the bedrooms?"

As Joey herded Bazarov and Maks to the master bedroom, Faisal laid the three pistols on the kitchen table. "I am waiting for ballistics reports, but I trust that your account of the incident will match the evidence. Am I correct to do so?"

"You are, Faisal," Liam said. "It went down just like we told you."

Faisal raised his bushy eyebrows. "I find that is rarely the case. But for now I must trust you, based on my past experience." He sat back in his chair. "Killing a man is a very serious business in Tunisia."

"It's serious to me no matter where it happens," Liam said.

"However, this Dvorkin seems like a very bad man. We are getting many reports from Interpol about him. There may still be charges filed, you understand."

Aidan looked from Faisal to Liam. His partner's face was impassive as he said, "I understand. I take full responsibility for my actions."

"You may not leave the country until this is resolved. That may restrict your ability to take on new clients."

Liam looked at Aidan. "We'll be in Bizerte for the next five weeks," he said. "So we won't be taking any new clients until then."

"We are in agreement then." Faisal closed the folder in front of him. "I will call you for further questioning." He stood up and reached out to shake Liam's hand. "It is good to know you are here in Tunisia."

"Thank you, Faisal. It's good to know you are here too."

Faisal turned to Aidan. "Salaam aleikum. I hope the next time we meet, there are no dead bodies involved."

"Aleikum salaam," Aidan said. "I hope so too."

When Faisal had gone, they let Joey, Bazarov, and Maks out of the master bedroom. "We're good to go," Liam said.

Bazarov called a travel agent to find a flight back to Ashgabat. At the same time, Joey got on the phone himself to see how he could get back to his SEAL team.

Aidan looked at Liam. "I guess I should call Madame Abboud."

"Guess so. Hey, Maks, you and I are the only ones who don't have somebody to call. Want to show me how that video game works?"

He and Maks sat down on the sofa as Aidan dialed Madame Abboud. "Liam and I have taken care of the situation with Maks," he said. "I'll pick up my classes tomorrow morning."

"That is very good," she said. "Maks, he is all right?"

Aidan looked over to where Maks was laughing and pressing the game controller as he gleefully shot Liam's character. "Yes, he's fine."

By the time he had hung up, Bazarov had finished his call as well. "I have a flight tonight. I will call the hotel for a car to the airport."

"We can take you," Aidan said.

"I will make my recommendation for the Chinese company to build the pipeline as soon as I return to Ashgabat," Bazarov said. He opened his wallet and pulled out a wad of cash. "I think this will pay for the hotel and your expenses. Ullyanov made arrangements for your salary?"

"Yes. What will happen to him?"

"He will not work for me again. I am sure he has returned to Russia. I will let Popov deal with him."

Aidan had a feeling that was not going to go well for Ullyanov. But that wasn't his problem.

"Come, Maks," Bazarov said. "Walk along the beach with me."

Maks abandoned the video game, and he and his father left the villa. Through the sliding glass doors, Aidan saw Bazarov with his arm around his son's shoulders, pointing at something down the beach, the two of them laughing.

Joey finally got through to someone who could get him on a flight. "I'm on a transport plane out of Tunis tomorrow morning. You guys going to stay here tonight?"

"They haven't kicked us out yet, though they've certainly got grounds," Aidan said.

An hour later, Bazarov and Maks returned from their walk, and they all drove Bazarov to the airport to catch his flight. Maks volunteered to carry his father's bag. "You will wait for me?"

"You bet," Aidan said.

They watched the father and son walk into the airport together. "He really does love his son, doesn't he?" Liam asked.

"Yeah, he does." Aidan looked sidelong at Liam. He knew Liam hadn't had much of a relationship with his father, but they hadn't spoken much about it. He settled back in his seat as they waited. There would be time.

When Maks returned, Aidan said, "How about we get some dinner in Sidi Bou Said. Show Maks and Joey a little bit of Tunisia."

Everyone agreed. Sidi Bou Said was a resort town just down the beach from the hotel, a blue and white village perched on cliffs overlooking the Mediterranean. They parked at the base of the village and began climbing the winding cobblestone streets. Maks walked ahead with Liam, while Joey and Aidan walked together.

"Sorry we didn't get to show you much of Tunis," Aidan said.

"Hell, I had a better time doing this than I'd ever have sightseeing. I just wanted to hang out with Billy, anyway."

"Next time you come back, we'll figure out some more mellow activities. Maybe kite surfing or quad bikes. We did both of them in Djerba and had a great time."

"Sounds like a plan," Joey said.

They stopped for dinner at the Sidi Chebaane café, with its gorgeous view down to the Mediterranean. The adults toasted each other with glasses of Vieux Magon, the local red wine Aidan and Liam both liked, Maks chiming in with a can of soda. Liam and Joey told stories of their SEAL adventures, Maks listening openmouthed.

It was a great, relaxing evening, and as Liam drove them to the hotel, Aidan sat back against the seat and thought about returning to teaching the next day. There would be piles of papers to grade, torturous sentences to straighten out, verb tenses to match, and untold other errors. But he was looking forward to it nonetheless.

They sat out under the stars that night, finishing the bottle of wine and telling more stories. Maks and Joey went to sleep, and Aidan and Liam went back to the master bedroom. When Aidan came out of the bathroom, he saw that Liam had plugged his iPhone into the slot provided for it in the alarm clock.

"That's Al Jarreau, isn't it?" Aidan asked as the music began.

"Sure is. Come here." He opened his arms, and Aidan walked over and nestled against them. As the gentle sounds of Jarreau's music filled the room, he leaned his head against Liam's broad chest, and Liam wrapped his arms around Aidan's back.

They swayed together as Jarreau sang, "The sky's a blackboard high above you.

If a shooting star goes by, I'll use that star, to write I love you, a thousand times across the sky."

Liam leaned down and whispered the next line into Aidan's ear. "Should the teacher stand so near, my love?"

"You bet," Aidan said, looking up. They kissed and swayed together until long after the song had finished.

* * *

They checked out of the hotel shortly after nine and drove to the Tunis airport. Aidan pulled up at a private aviation terminal where Joey could meet up with his transport.

"I'm glad you came, bud," Liam said, hoisting Joey's duffel out of the back of the SUV.

"Me too." Joey opened his arms, and Liam stepped into them, hugging the big SEAL with an unself-conscious enthusiasm.

"You know, the planes fly up to Italy too," Joey said when they had backed away. "You and Aidan should come up for a visit."

"We'll do that."

Joey turned and walked away, and Liam got back in the front seat of the SUV. "Take us to Bizerte, driver," he said to Aidan, then reclined the seat.

Neil Plakcy

Neil Plakcy has loved romance novels since he began reading his mother's Harlequins as a teenager. He is a three-time Lambda Literary Award Finalist and author of the Mahu series of police procedural novels set in Hawaii, featuring gay homicide detective Kimo Kanapa'aka (*Mahu, Mahu Surfer, Mahu Fire* and *Mahu Vice*). His short erotic fiction, including many stories about Kimo, has appeared in nearly 20 anthologies, and he has also edited two anthologies himself—*Hard Hats* and *Surfer Boys*. His romance novels are *Three Wrong Turns in the Desert, Dancing with the Tide,* and *Guardian Angel of South Beach* (Loose Id), and *GayLife.com* (MLR Press). He is a graduate of the University of Pennsylvania, Columbia University, and Florida International University, where he received his MFA in creative writing. He lives in South Florida with his partner and their golden retriever.

Loose Id® Titles by Neil Plakcy

Available in digital format at www.loose-id.com and other retailers

Guardian Angel of South Beach
Mi Amor

* * * *

The HAVE BODY WILL GUARD Series
Three Wrong Turns in the Desert
Dancing with the Tide
Teach Me Tonight

Available in print at your favorite bookseller

Mi Amor

* * * *

The HAVE BODY WILL GUARD Series
Three Wrong Turns in the Desert
Dancing with the Tide
Teach Me Tonight

CPSIA information can be obtained at www.ICGtesting.com
Printed in the USA
LVOW131017270113

317405LV00003B/355/P